FIRST COMES LOVE

A PRIDE OREGON NOVEL

JILL SANDERS

GRAYTON

This is a work of fiction. Names, characters, places, and incidents either are the product of the author's imagination or are used fictitiously, and any resemblance to actual persons, living or dead, business establishments, events or locales is entirely coincidental.

FIRST COMES LOVE

DIGITAL ISBN: 978-1-945100-22-2

PRINT ISBN: 979-8-672027-65-4

Text copyright © 2020 Grayton Press

Copyeditor: Erica Ellis – inkdeepediting.com

SUMMARY

Head back to Pride Oregon to find out what some of your favorite Jill Sanders' characters are up to.

Rose jumps at the chance to be the architect of a big project in the only town she's ever dreamed of living in. She thinks this could be her chance at happiness, until she realizes that the Jordans have put Jacob in charge of the project. Why did the man infuriate her? It couldn't be the fact that she's been secretly crushing on him all her life.

Jacob is hired by his uncle to oversee an exciting new project that could save the town of Pride. Unfortunately, that means working closely with the one person that he is completely infatuated with. It is ironic that she is the only person who can't stand him. Fighting with Rose is almost second nature. After all, it's one of the reasons he fell for her in the first place.

PROLOGUE

Rose stomped her feet as she marched back to the cabin to tell her daddy what Jacob Jordan had done this time. How was she supposed to spend a whole summer with that gross boy following her around like a... booger?

By the time she reached the cabin with the red door, which was where she and her mommy and daddy were staying this year, big fat tears were rolling down her chubby cheeks.

Being nine was hard. Especially when she was the outsider among all the kids she was stuck playing with for the whole stupid summer. Oh, she liked most of the Jordan kids. Suzie, Riley, and Lilly were among her bestest friends. Sara, Suzie's older sister, always looked out for her. Well, usually.

Today was the exception. Sara had been busy helping Riley untangle her hair from the fishing net her brother had tossed in the shallow water to catch minnows when Jacob had snuck up and... She sniffled again and wiped at the tears as she remembered what the bully had done.

Jacob Jordan was a goober. He was two years older than

her and about a foot taller too, which in his mind meant that he was the boss of her.

She was just a baby, or so he kept telling her each time they were alone.

She stomped her feet on each stair she climbed on the front deck to the little cabin and pushed her way through the front door. She rushed into her daddy's arms.

The fact that her daddy was fast asleep on the sofa didn't register until she'd flung her body on top of his.

"Daddy!" she cried.

Instantly, her father's arms wrapped around her.

"What's wrong baby?" His deep voice helped to soothe her even more.

"J-J-J-Jacob Jordan is a booger." She cried into her father's chest, soaking his shirt. Her voice was muffled, and she knew he wasn't really able to understand her as she quickly told her story, but she didn't care.

Her father's chuckle stopped the tears almost instantly. Pulling back, she looked up into his eyes as she stuck out her bottom lip.

"He pushed me," she said again. "And then chased me with a big booger thing."

His father laughed again, making her even angrier.

She crossed her little arms over her chest, a move she'd learned from her mother, and narrowed her eyes as anger continued to grow in her.

"Honey, I'm sure it was just a slug. And that's what little boys do to little girls they like." Her father brushed a hand down her long dark hair.

"Nuh-uh." She shook her head. "Jacob Jordan says he hates me and that he's the boss of me." She shook her hair, dislodging her father's hand.

Her father continued to smile at her. "Well," he said

after clearing his throat, "did you tell him that girls are always the boss of boys?"

She sniffled and frowned. "They are?"

Her father's smile grew. "Yes. Take a look at your mom and I..."

"Mommy's the boss of you?" she asked, dropping her arms to her sides.

"Well, when I want to have burgers for dinner and your mother wants spaghetti, where do we go eat?"

"The spaghetti place," she answered, causing her father to laugh and nod.

"That's because she's the boss." He tucked a strand of her long dark hair behind her ear. "And when I told you that you couldn't spend the night with Riley and Lilly last week, what happened?"

"Mommy said I could." She wiped her eyes as she started to see the trend. "Are we the boss of every boy?"

Her father laughed. "No, just boys that chase you with slugs," he added quickly.

She thought about it and nodded. "I don't wanna be the boss of Conner or George. They're too busy playing fort or swimming. I don't like playing fort, and I'm not supposta swim without you there."

"Right." Her father's smile slipped slightly. "So, are you okay?"

"Yeah." She wiped her face and then climbed off his lap. "I'm going to take a juice and a cookie." She walked to the small kitchen.

"You better not. It might spoil your dinner," her father said. She glanced over her shoulder and lifted her dark eyebrows at him and then smiled.

"I'm going to take a juice and a cookie." She waited, and her father laughed.

"Just one, okay? I wouldn't want your mommy to get upset at me." He lowered his voice as if she were around instead of in town shopping with Megan and Lacey today. "Because Mommy is the ultimate boss in our house."

Rose thought about it and nodded. "One cookie for you and one for me." She took two cookies from the container.

"That sounds just right." Her father pulled her into his lap again.

"But Jacob Jordan better not come after me with a booger again," she added before taking a big bite of the cookie. "Or I'm gonna slug him next time."

Her father laughed.

CHAPTER ONE

Fourteen Years later....

Rose stood at the base of the hillside and glanced up into the sunlight at the large machinery moving slowly down towards her. The smell of asphalt and oil somehow made her dreams feel more real.

For the past six months she'd been working her ass off on Hidden Cove. Designing six unique homes, each with multiple elevations and flooring options, which met all of the state and county codes and regulations was no small feat.

She'd been thankful for Blake Jordan's help in narrowing down basic options like flooring colors and lighting options. She'd even helped her find local subcontractors to supply all those products. Putting packets together for new buyers to choose from hadn't been hard because each supplier had willingly given her samples of each option. It had taken her almost three weeks, working one on one with Blake. Blake was Matthew's wife and a fairly new mother of an adorable girl, Georgia, which meant that they either held their meetings at Blake's house while the little girl was either happily entertained or sleeping, or over at Rose's parents' summer home.

Shortly after her eleventh birthday, Rose's parents had finally purchased a home on the north side of the small town of Pride.

The massive three-bedroom spread had been more like a home sometimes than the townhouse in Los Angeles, the apartment in New York, or the massive mansion they had in Portland that they had bounced between most of her childhood.

After all, Pride had been a steady place they returned to on a regular basis.

She had always loved the layout of the cabin, as her parents called the three-thousand square foot home that sat on its very own private cove.

She'd spent her childhood sketching and resketching the layout of the home until she could close her eyes and mentally walk through the place no matter where she was.

When she wasn't there, she'd dream about being there and when she was there, she'd wish their visit would last forever.

She loved every part of the home, including its large finished basement complete with a long bar that sat ten people, a cozy home movie theater, and, one of its best features, an outdoor jacuzzi. It even had a pool table in the basement, and she'd spent countless hours playing with her parents. She'd spent so much time at the pool table that her father swore she'd be able to beat any pool shark she went up against.

The upstairs was just as impressive to her as a child. The home boasted high wood ceilings that she used to love looking up at while listening to a fire crackle in the massive two-story stone fireplace. Windows sat on either side of the fireplace and looked out to a deck, which in turn looked out over their small grassy yard. There was a pathway that led down to the private cove, which was perfect for summer swimming.

Her father had at one point built a tree swing for her along the pathway, which she had tested out the first week she'd returned to Pride.

The first summer they'd moved in, she had been so excited that she would finally be freed from the hold of her arch nemesis. Or so she'd thought. There was no escaping Jacob Jordan and the tricks he liked to play on her back then.

Each summer when she returned to Pride, Jacob's tricks and teasing were just as steady and constant as the fact that she would have to return to Portland come school time.

But when Todd Jordan had offered her the job of a lifetime as head designer and developer for a new subdivision he was developing in Pride, Hidden Cove, she'd jumped at the chance to move to Pride full-time. She'd taken over her parents' summer home less than a week after getting his call.

It wasn't until after her first meeting with Todd that she realized she'd be working full-time with Jacob.

She remembered walking into the offices at Jordan Shipping in downtown Pride and being so excited about the opportunity she'd given Todd Jordan a hug. After all, the man was like an uncle to her. She couldn't remember a time when she hadn't known him and the rest of the Jordan clan.

"Rose, my god, you get more beautiful and grown up every time I see you." Todd had chuckled and held onto her.

"I can't thank you enough for giving me this chance," she'd said to him.

"Don't mention it. From what your parents tell me, you

were top of your design class." He motioned for her to sit down.

"Yes." She shifted slightly and then completely froze when Jacob walked into the office and sat across from her.

It had been almost two years since she'd seen him last. In that time, he'd grown even more handsome than he'd been before. His dark hair still held a slight curl to it. The fact that she'd always dreamed of running her fingers through it irritated her since she knew what kind of person he was underneath all the muscle and the toned perfect skin.

He'd grown a full scruffy beard that he kept trimmed neat, the kind of look most women would go crazy over. She tried to exclude herself from that group, but just seeing him had her knees turning to jelly.

Even with him fully dressed in one of his signature flannel shirts, she could tell he'd filled out with a bunch of new muscles since the last time she'd seen him.

Jacob was easily as tall as Conner, his older brother, yet that was where the similarities seemed to end. Jacob's twin sister, Riley, looked absolutely nothing like the two brothers. In fact, the one person Jacob looked most like was his uncle Todd. Sure, he had his father Iian's height and his mother Allison's eyes, but the rest of him matched his uncle almost perfectly.

She'd wanted to ask Todd what Jacob was doing there, but then Todd had informed her that Jacob was going to be the project manager in charge of overseeing and organizing all the construction.

Which meant that she'd taken a job that would require her to work very closely with her sworn enemy for the next few years.

Now, months and more arguments than she cared to

count later, she wondered if she would have turned the job down had she known ahead of time about the requirement to work with Jacob.

But facts were facts. She was tied to the job now and, to be honest, it was the best career choice she'd made thus far.

Finishing her core college classes when she'd still been in high school had been easy for her. Deciding what to do for a career had been a little more difficult of a decision. Then one day her mother had brought up the sketches that Rose had been drawing all of her life. For as long as she could remember, Rose had been tracing or drawing homes, ones she'd been in and ones she'd dreamed up herself.

So she'd enrolled in classes that would further her love of all things architecture. Less than a month after graduating with her five-year degree, she'd gotten the call from the Jordans and moved back to Pride.

Now, as she moved out of the way of the machinery that was laying down the roads to the subdivision that she'd designed herself, she couldn't help but feel proud of the path she'd taken.

Everything was going just as she'd planned.

"Lookin' good, Derby." Just hearing Jacob Jordan's voice had her back teeth grinding together.

She glanced over to see the man walking towards her. His standard uniform of blue jeans, work boots, and some sort of flannel shirt looked too damn good on the man she'd grown up loathing. Okay, loathing was too strong of a word. Despising. There, that was a better word.

She didn't hate Jacob Jordan. Not really. But she did believe that it was the man's life mission to annoy her.

From small decisions such as picking out which hammer to purchase to larger things such as determining where to put the clubhouse in the subdivision, they seemed to always butt heads.

"Yes, yes it does." She crossed her arms over her chest and smiled as she took the compliment, even though he hadn't technically given her one.

"Too bad everyone enjoying the clubhouse and other amenities will miss out on the amazing views up there." He stopped beside her and mimicked her stance as they both looked up the hillside.

"And there it is." She sighed as she reached up and rubbed the base of her nose, trying desperately to work through the headache she had been fighting all morning.

"What?" Jacob asked, glancing at her.

"You can't give a simple compliment. You have to add an insult every single time," she said, motioning to the view in front of them.

"What insult?" He frowned over at her.

"Seriously?" She groaned and threw her hands up in the air, then turned around and stormed back into the construction trailer she'd been sharing with him for the past month or so.

"Hey." He followed her inside, not caring to knock off the mud from his boots. "There wasn't an insult in my statement."

"Really?" She tilted her head at him and briefly took in his rugged good looks, his muscular build, his damn sexy lips that she'd dreamed of kissing for her entire life. Shaking those thoughts from her mind, she snapped back to reality. "I understand that you think the clubhouse, gym, swimming pool, and tennis courts should have been at the very top of the property, but there is something to be said from having them closer to the base of the hill." She held up her hand as he watched her. "The bedrock is more stable for pools and tennis court surfaces, and the extra fee we will get for each lot with an amazing view outweighs people not being able to enjoy the view while swimming or hitting a few balls around. Not to mention the cost deficit of building such large structures on level ground."

She'd noticed the corners of his mouth curve upward the more she talked, which somehow made her even more agitated.

"I wasn't trying to tear you down. After some extra consideration and going over the numbers, I'm in agreement with your assessments," he said, leaning on the edge of his desk with his ankles crossed.

She moved closer to him and narrowed her eyes at him. "I'm waiting," she said, cautiously.

His eyebrows shot up. "For?"

"The punch line." She moved a little closer to him.

He chuckled softly and shrugged. "Guess there isn't one this time."

She remained silent as she scanned his face, looking for any sign of deceit.

"What's wrong with you?" she asked suddenly.

Her statement caused him to laugh again.

"Maybe I'm just trying to tell you that I'm impressed," he answered after a moment. "I can see by that look you're giving me that you don't believe me." He sighed. "Listen, I just think... It's just..." He ran his hand through his hair, a move she'd seen a million times on him and knew signaled that he was frustrated. About what, she still didn't know.

Jacob Jordan had never looked at Rose as anything other than a little sister, the type to annoy. Or so she believed. That was up until the moment he reached for her and pulled her into his arms. Even then, when his lips pushed up against hers, her mind went completely blank.

Before the kiss had really registered with her, she heard the door to the trailer open and close again quickly. Jacob pushed her away and rushed to sit behind his desk just before Conner stepped inside followed by a woman that she'd seen several times in town. It was either Robin or her sister Kara. The two sisters looked so much alike to her and since she hadn't officially been introduced to either of them, she wasn't sure who was who yet.

Before she had time to recover from Jacob's kiss, she was quickly introduced to Kara Jenkins as what had just transpired between her and Jacob started to sink in. She half listened as Conner explained that Kara's parents were moving to Pride and looking for a home, then she woke up and jumped into action.

For the next two hours, she turned on her best salesman face. She was happily surprised when Conner let them know that he too was going to be purchasing a home from them.

By the end of the day, she was so excited at the first two homes sales that Jacob's kiss had fallen to the sidelines. But that night, when she was lying in bed alone, her body remembered every second of the most wonderful kiss she'd ever had.

CHAPTER TWO

Jacob Jordan was screwed. Why the hell had he listened to his brother?

Conner had mentioned in passing that he believed that Rose had a crush on him, and it had been in the forefront of Jacob's mind the entire time she'd been arguing with him about...well, he couldn't remember what she'd been upset at him for this time.

So, naturally, he'd kissed her.

He had recovered quickly when Conner and Kara had shown up on the job site unannounced.

It had been stupid for him to make the move. Even dumber to do it on the job site where at any moment a worker could catch them.

How unprofessional and desperate could he get?

Now that he'd had plenty of time to think about it, he realized that Rose hadn't responded to his kiss. Like, at all. She had held very still and had acted completely unfazed by his touch. Which obviously meant that his brother had been way off.

There was no way anyone who was a little into someone else would respond like that. She would have acted differently if she were the slight bit interested. Right?

So, he turned his mind back to his work. Managing and coordinating the workers was a full-time task, especially when it appeared that Rose was going out of her way to be annoyed at every decision he made.

Then again, he'd spent his entire life going out of his way to annoy her. Even so, he couldn't remember a time in his life that he hadn't loved her.

Since the first moments he could remember thinking about girls in that light, Rose had been the one in his mind. The one he'd planned on marrying, the one he'd wanted to be with.

He'd loved teasing her and getting her to notice him. She was perfect, even when he'd made her mad. God, he loved those times—she looked even prettier when she was angry.

He always looked forward to the summers, when he knew her family would return to Pride and he'd be able to see her again. Throughout high school, he'd dated, but he'd always broken things off with whomever he was seeing weeks before summer would start. He'd never wanted to be tied to anyone else when Rose showed up.

He'd dreamed of making a move on her all of his life. Thoughts of sweeping her off her feet with some grandiose romantic gesture or showing her a passionate night on the beach had played over in his mind.

Never had he imagined he'd be so smooth as to attack her in the construction trailer while the pair of them had been muddy and tired from a long day's work. Real smooth, Jordan. Could he be a bigger fool?

For the next few days, he tried to focus on his work and push his temporary lapse of judgment out of his mind. Even when he'd been sitting across from her enjoying a family dinner, he kept his mind off of the kiss. He'd been too embarrassed to look directly into her eyes for fear that she'd laugh at him.

He'd been doing a great job of putting it in the past, but then his mother had requested that he drive Rose home. Rose had ridden with his folks to the dinner up at his twin sister and her husband's place, and his mother insisted that she was too tired to drive Rose all the way back home.

"Mom," he warned her in a low tone, "are you trying to set me up?"

Allison Jordan looked shocked. "Me? I would never do such a thing." She sighed as she reached up and touched her temple. "No, I'm just tired and after the exciting news that I'm going to finally be a grandmother..." His mother's smile brightened. "I'm going to be a grandmother," she repeated. He felt his own heart skip at the thought of his twin, Riley, having a baby. It was still so... unreal in his mind. "Anyway, with all of the excitement, it might be easier if you took Rose home."

"Sure," he said after seeing weariness in his mother's eyes. She did look tired. Happy, but tired. "Go home." He kissed her on the cheek and used sign language to say good-night to his father. "Get some rest," he finished saying to his mother.

"Well," he said when he found Rose talking with Blake in the kitchen, "looks like you're stuck riding home with me. My folks just left and asked me to take you back to your place." He waited for the argument he knew was bound to follow.

He was slightly shocked to see her nod her head quickly. "I'll be ready to go soon," she said softly.

"No rush," he told her. "I'm going to go congratulate my sister again." He scanned the space for Riley before leaving the two women to finish talking.

Finding his twin wrapped in her husband's arms, he cleared his throat until the pair glanced over at him.

Riley looked nothing like him or anyone else in his family. Actually, the person she reminded him most of was his aunt Lacey. Riley was short for a Jordan at only five-foot-four. Her bleached blonde hair had darkened a few shades, but it was still her signature look. The only hint that they were related was the Jordan smile and blue eyes.

"That's how you two kids got in this mess in the first place," Jacob joked.

Carter chuckled before leaning down and placing another kiss on Riley's lips. "I'm going to start cleaning up." Carter shook his hand.

"Congratulations," he said to his brother-in-law again.

"Thanks," Carter replied before turning to leave.

He saw Riley rest her hands over her flat belly. His twin was so much smaller than he was that when she walked into his arms, he could rest his chin on the top of her head.

"You're going to be a mom," he said softly.

He felt her sigh and then chuckle. "I am," she said against his chest. "Can you believe it?"

"Not yet." He glanced down at her. "But the moment you start getting fat…" She pinched his side and had him chuckling. "You're going to be a great mom," he added somberly.

Her smile slipped a little as she looked up at him. "You're going to be an amazing uncle."

He nodded. "What can I do to help you guys clean up?" He glanced around.

"Nothing. Carter and Corey have this."

He noticed that the twin brothers were rushing around and had already cleared most of the mess up. Where Riley and he looked nothing alike, Carter and Corey were identical, and it was sometimes difficult to tell them apart.

"Go home," she said softly. "It's starting to rain, and Mom told me you're driving Rose home." His sister's eyes sparkled with mischief.

"Was that idea your doing?" he asked, knowing full well the look his sister got when she was meddling in his life.

Riley had always tried to set him up. The first time had been back in grade school with Stephany Wilkinson, whom he'd dated for all of two days.

"Me?" Riley touched a finger to her chest. "No, I would never do such a thing."

He laughed. "Right. Mom said the exact same thing." He narrowed his eyes at her. "Rose and I..."

"What?" Rose said from directly behind him.

He winced and then turned around to see Rose standing in the doorway with her arms crossed over her chest, glaring at him.

He cleared his throat before finishing. "Are going to head out because the rain is getting worse."

He could tell that Rose wasn't buying his diversion from what he'd been about to say, but she sighed and walked over to hug Riley.

"Thank you for dinner. Congratulations again," Rose said to his sister.

Five minutes later, he was driving them down the hill towards Pride. The Derby summer home sat on the outskirts of town on the opposite side of town from Riley and Carter's place, which happened to be on the same side of town as his parents' place.

The drive seemed to stretch out since the truck was filled with silence. Awkward silence. In all the years he'd known Rose, they had never had an awkward silence before. He didn't like it.

"So," he said after clearing his throat, "babies." He glanced sideways at her, thinking about his sister and his cousin Lilly announcing that they were both pregnant over dinner that evening. "Who could've seen that coming."

Rose shrugged slightly. "That usually happens after a couple gets married."

"Well, sure." He turned off the side road and started heading through town. "I mean, yeah. But..." He felt totally stupid. "It's just kind of crazy that I'm going to be an uncle."

"Must be nice. Being an only child, I never really had that option."

"Why didn't your parents ever have more kids?" he asked her.

She shrugged. "They wanted to, but apparently after I was born, my mother's health didn't allow for it. She'd been shot before they had been married."

"She had?" he asked, jerking the wheel slightly. He'd known Roberta Derby, or Rob as everyone called her, his entire life. The woman was the epitome of health.

"What happened?" he asked.

"She was a cop." He'd known that already about Rose's mother but remained silent. Rose was looking out of the window as she started talking. "Someone had broken into my dad's art store and had stolen a lot of art and killed a man who worked there. My mother was the lead detective on the case. In the process of catching the killer, they fell in love and, well, she ended up getting shot saving my father's life. I guess the bullet almost nicked her heart. Anyway, when she was pregnant with me, the doctor hinted that it wouldn't be a good idea to go through another childbirth." She shrugged. "There for a while, they thought about adopting."

"Why didn't they?" He pulled into the long driveway at her place.

"I'm not sure." She shrugged as he parked by her truck. "I know they tried once, but the pregnant mother of the child they were trying to adopt changed her mind before the baby was born. I think it took a mental toll on my parents."

"I can't imagine going through something like that. Getting excited about welcoming a new child into your home and then losing the opportunity." He sighed and rested his head back. "My parents were lucky in that sense, I suppose."

"Still, they weren't without their challenges. Your father losing his hearing must have been difficult for a young couple." She glanced over at him.

Jacob shrugged. "It happened long before they started dating. My father was eighteen when the boat accident that took his hearing and killed my grandfather happened."

"It did? For some reason I was thinking your parents were already together before then." She shook her head.

He glanced over at her and ran his eyes over her face. Had there ever been a time he hadn't dreamed of being with her like this?

He didn't know what possessed him to reach over and take her hand in his. He felt her tense for a split second, then relax.

"They had known each other their entire lives," he said softly, thinking about how in some way his and Rose's lives mirrored his parents' lives. "Then my mom moved away to the city to work with your dad." He smiled. "My dad often mentions how he'd believed at one point that they were more than friends."

"Really?" Rose shook her head. "No way. My dad often says he thinks of her like she's a little sister, like my aunt Katie."

He nodded. "Yeah, there for a while, I believed your dad was one of my uncles."

Rose chuckled. "That would have made that kiss the other day even more awkward," she said, then he surmised that she instantly regretted it.

He looked down at their joined hands. "Speaking of that kiss..."

"Don't." She tried to tug her hand free, but he stopped her.

"Rose." He pulled her hand up between them. "We've known each other our entire lives. I don't want things to be strained between us. I should've never kissed you. Call it a moment of weakness."

She was silent for a while. "Weakness?"

He sighed and rested his head back and closed his eyes again. "I won't apologize for it." He turned to her again. "Only because I'd been dreaming of doing it long before then."

She sucked her bottom lip between her teeth as she ran her eyes over him. When she glanced down to look at his mouth, he held in a groan.

Was she thinking about kissing him again? Did she want him to kiss her? If he kissed her now, would she respond to his touch this time?

He was spared questioning things even further when she rushed across the space between them and laid her lips over his.

His heart actually stopped beating for a moment as his brain caught up with what was going on.

Then his hands moved to circle her, pulling her closer as his instincts took over.

Her body was plastered against his as she moved her mouth slowly over his. When he tasted her on his tongue, a low moan escaped his lips.

Somehow, she'd ended up in his lap and when she started grinding her hips against him, he realized just how out of control he was. An image of taking her here, now, in his truck as the rain pelted the windshield, flooded his mind.

It took all his will to pull back away from her. Her tight, sexy body was still pressed up against his, and he had to close his eyes and take several calming breaths before he could get himself back under control. It didn't help that her scent and taste were filling his senses, surrounding him.

When he opened his eyes, Rose was looking down at him as if trying to figure him out.

"There is nothing I want more than to continue this..." he started, and he felt her entire body tense as she moved to climb off him.

His hands went up to her hips and held her there.

"Just give me a minute," he begged, but she tugged free and was already climbing off him and was reaching for the door handle. "Rose." He moved to take her hand again, but she yanked it out of his grasp.

"It's fine," she said, avoiding his eyes. "I get it."

"Do you?" he asked, stopping her from opening the door.

Her eyes turned towards him, and he could see the heat and the hurt behind them.

"Yes," she almost spat at him. "You were just toying with me. Again," she blurted out.

He raised his eyebrows.

"The hell I was," he was about to say but before he could respond, she climbed out of the truck and dashed through the rain to the house.

Hell. That had not gone well.

CHAPTER THREE

Rose was such an idiot. Over the next few weeks, she kept her head down and avoided Jacob whenever possible. Of course, that was easier said than done since they were crammed together in the small construction trailer and had to work with one another on a daily basis.

Still, when Kara's parents visited and signed a contract on their new home, she was able to keep busy outside of Jacob's presence.

She even found it refreshing to work with Conner and Kara to help them pick out all the options on their new home. She hadn't known at first if Conner and Kara were officially a couple, even though they had attended the dinner at Riley and Carter's together. Then she'd heard that Kara had moved in with Conner and on more than one occasion saw them having dinner together at the Golden Oar when she'd decided not to cook for herself, which happened roughly twice a week. She usually ended up either at the Golden Oar or at Baked, the town's only pizzeria, owned by Carter and Corey Miller.

Sitting in a restaurant and eating dinner alone hadn't

really bothered her, as she'd had her work to keep her company.

Tonight, she was sitting in a corner booth near the large fireplace at the Golden Oar when Jacob plopped down across from her looking haggard.

"Problem?" she asked, a little annoyed that he'd interrupted her work. She'd been reworking the numbers for the Jenkins' options in order to get a budget to them by Monday.

"Didn't you hear?" he said, waving a waitress over to the table.

"Hear?" she asked, shutting her laptop. She doubted that she'd get any more work done with Jacob at the table. "Hear what?"

"Where have you been all day?" he asked her after ordering a coke and a burger.

"Working." She frowned. "Why?"

He leaned closer to her. "Someone shot Kara."

"What?" she gasped. "Is she okay?" Worry flooded her about the woman she was slowly becoming friends with.

"She just got out of surgery about an hour ago. Everyone's been down at the hospital waiting for word on her." Jacob relaxed back in the booth.

"What happened?" she asked, shaking her head as she tried to imagine anyone wanting to harm Kara.

"She was walking from their apartment to work when someone in a blue truck drove by and shot her in the head and the arm. The first bullet grazed her here." He ran his finger just above his ear. "The second one tore through her left arm. The doctor says she'll make a full recovery but may need some physical therapy."

"Did they catch the guy? Why did he shoot her?" Then it hit her. "Blue truck? The same one that spewed rocks at them up on the job site?" she asked, remembering that first day they'd visited and how someone on their jobsite had almost run down Conner and Kara.

Jacob frowned. "Appears so. No, they haven't found him yet, but they think it has something to do with Thomas Carson."

"The developer your uncle purchased the land out from under?" she asked after thinking about where she'd heard that name before. She'd remembered hearing the story of how the developer had started an illegal gambling ring in town last year and had done a few other shady things to try and lower the price of the land around Pride. Land which Todd had turned around and quickly purchased at fair market value from the owners, undermining the man's plans.

"Yeah," Jacob said after his drink and her food arrived. He reached over and took a French fry from her plate, and she held back from swatting his hand away, remembering that he'd sat in the hospital all day. "I was at the hospital waiting for news about Kara all day long and didn't grab lunch or dinner," he explained, making her feel even more annoyed that he knew her so well as to understand what she'd been thinking.

Instead of being upset at him sharing her fries, she shrugged and pushed her plate towards him.

"Didn't you wonder why I wasn't at work today?" he asked between fries.

She shrugged. "Not really. I guess I just thought you were somewhere on the site." She had been busy herself but had noticed that he hadn't been at work and figured he'd eventually show up.

"What about the news all over town? Surely someone you bumped into today mentioned the shooting?" he asked.

She shrugged again. The truth was, she'd been so preoccupied with work, she hadn't even talked to anyone outside of a few contractors.

"Either way," he said after a moment, "Kara's in recovery and Conner is there with her. Something tells me she's going to be planning another wedding soon," he said with a chuckle.

"You think your brother's going to propose?" she asked.

"You should have seen his face." He shook his head and for a moment looked so concerned that she felt the urge to reach across the table and take his hand. "I've only ever seen that look on my dad's face, when one of us would end up in the ER with a broken bone." He waited until his burger was delivered. "Thanks, Steph," he said to the waitress, and then took a big bite. "I'm pretty sure that my dear brother is gone completely. Hook, line, and sinker." He chuckled.

"That's wonderful news." She pulled her plate back towards her and took another bite of her own burger. "I always wondered about those two."

"Yeah," Jacob said through his food. She gave him a look to warn him to not talk with his mouth full, and he immediately shut it. He finished talking when he was done swallowing. "I guess there will be one less Jordan bachelor around town soon. The ladies will be highly disappointed."

"Oh?" She took a drink of the beer she'd ordered and had been nursing since she'd sat down almost an hour earlier. "I didn't know there was a line of women biding their time for a chance with one of the great Jordan men." She fluttered her eyelashes. "And here I am squandering a romantic dinner with one of the last highly sought-after available bachelors in Pride."

He crossed his eyes and stuck out his tongue in such a Jacob move that she laughed.

"There it is. There's the sex appeal and sophistication all women desire in a man," she added before taking a sip of her beer.

They both smiled and joked as they finished their meal together. She couldn't remember having a more fun time with Jacob. Ever.

It was so unlike him to not tease or rile her up that she almost forgot who she was sitting across the table from. That was until she mentioned that she had better get going home because her workdays started pretty early.

"Yeah." He chuckled. "I hear your boss is a real douche and complains when you arrive late."

"My..." She narrowed her eyes. "You mean your uncle? My boss?" she said slowly.

It was a long-standing rift between them. Jacob kept insisting that he was officially her boss since he was the project manager and she was the designer and developer, a job that he figured fell under him.

She, on the other hand, kept insisting that Todd had made it clear to her that they would be working together as equals. She knew for a fact that people in their roles usually worked side by side for most projects.

Jacob shrugged and had one of those cocky smiles he normally got when he was going to say something arrogant.

"I mean the one who manages everyone." He leaned back and crossed his arms behind his head.

"Oh." She leaned forward and smiled. "Like the developer?"

"No, the developer develops. The project manager..." he started, but when she groaned and rolled her eyes, he stopped.

"Doesn't it get old?" she broke in.

"What?" he asked, running his eyes over her.

"The ego? The superiority complex." She tilted her head slightly as she watched him.

"Didn't you know that all Jordan men are filled with pride?" he asked her with a smile.

"You forget"—she leaned even closer and lowered her voice—"that I've known you all of your life. You weren't always so full of yourself." She smiled as she remembered one warm summer night when Jacob's older brother and cousins had played a trick on him. "I seem to remember one summer when you'd been tricked into thinking that big foot was real and living in one of the old cabins along the coast. I believe you even were tricked into making the trek out to said cabin one night where your cousins thoroughly scared the piss out of you."

Jacob was silent for a moment before breaking out into laughter. "That was a good one." He smiled over at her. "You have to admit, the dummy they dressed in one of my great-grandmother's fur coats was a little over the top. Still, very effective."

"I can't believe all of the tricks you used to play on one another," she said with a shake of her head.

"Me?" He motioned to his chest. "What about the ones you used to play on us? I seem to remember you had a few good ones you did on my sister and Lilly. Each summer I'd sit back and wait to see what schemes you had in store for them."

"They started it," she said with a smile, remembering all the ploys Riley and Lilly used to pull on her and how many she would come up with in return. They were harmless, petty little jokes that usually made everyone laugh. Not like the ones Jacob had pulled on her each year.

But the more she thought back, the more she realized all of his tricks had been much of the same type that she and his cousins had pulled on each other. But because it had been Jacob pulling them on her, she'd taken them more to heart. Because her heart had been so shielded towards him, every little betrayal had stung three-fold.

His smile fell away. "You had family. You just didn't know it," he said softly.

Her heart warmed at that thought. How many times had she thought the very same thing since the last summer she and her family had visited Pride together?

It wasn't difficult to see as an adult that the Jordans had treated her like family all along. And for the most part, she'd been right there treating them as the same. All except Jacob Jordan.

Jacob had always been and would always be more to her. Even if he would never know.

"I guess I did," she said, feeling suddenly weary.

"I'll walk you out," he said, standing up quickly.

It was as if he'd read her thoughts about not wanting to discuss it further. She realized he often knew her mind and, this time, it didn't annoy her like it had before. Instead, it warmed her heart even more knowing that they understood each other so much that they didn't have to vocalize some of the basics.

Stepping out in the fresh snow, she took a deep breath and let the cold ocean air wash over her.

"We'll have snow for Halloween," he said beside her.

"It won't stop the kids from enjoying the night." She thought of the handful of young kids that lived on her street and remembered how she'd always wished she could remain in Pride for the holiday seasons.

"No, it never does," he agreed as they stopped by her truck.

When he reached up and brushed a large snowflake from her hair, her breath caught.

Just remembering the way his mouth had felt against hers, how his muscles had felt under her fingertips, caused her insides to heat and vibrate.

He moved a step closer and, once again, her body responded as it always did when he was so close to her.

"Fresh snow on a Rose," he said softly before bending down and laying his lips over hers.

CHAPTER FOUR

He didn't know what had caused him to kiss Rose again. Maybe it was because he'd spent an entire day watching his brother worry over the health and well-being of the woman he loved.

Maybe it was watching the fresh snow in Rose's hair for the first time. Most of the memories he had of her were filled with swimsuits, shorts, and summer fun. But here, in the midst of one of the first snowfalls of the winter, he couldn't believe how beautiful she was. He allowed himself to let go once again.

This time he was in control of the kiss and marveled at the instant response Rose had given him. She'd pulled him closer and run her gloved hands through his hair.

He pinned her body between his and her truck as he enjoyed the taste of her lips.

When a car honked its horn at them, he pulled back as he remembered where they were.

"Rose," he sighed and rested his forehead against hers. "I'm not toying with you." His eyes locked with hers. "I would never do that. I've wanted to kiss you for as long as I can remember. Honest."

She nodded slightly. "I..." Her eyes moved off his and then she motioned towards her truck. "I'd better get going."

She tried to turn but realized he was still blocking her in. He wanted to remain where he was, holding her, kissing her, but instead, he stepped back and helped her into the truck by taking her arm.

She glanced back at him, her dark eyebrow raised.

"Sorry," he mumbled. "It's icy out here," he explained, stepping back further.

"Tell Conner when you see him that I'm happy Kara's okay," she told him.

"Will do. Kara should be home soon enough."

"Night," she said before shutting the door.

He watched her truck lights disappear down the street and decided he was too tired to weigh the pros and cons of their relationship at the moment.

Driving back to his parents' house, he realized that Conner had been smart to move into the apartment above the grocery store a while back.

Not that there wasn't a lot of privacy at his parents' house. The place was certainly big enough or had at least felt that way all of his childhood. But now that he was thinking about dating... Was he thinking about dating Rose?

That thought had him almost skidding off the road as he turned off the main street towards the cluster of Jordan homes.

At one point, the five individual homes on Beachview Drive had belonged to different families. But, over the years, his aunts and uncles had purchased every single place. They had all joked that someday they would change the name of the street to Jordan Drive.

Parking beside his mother's new SUV, he looked up at the massive house. When had he stopped thinking of the place as his home and started thinking of it as his parents' instead?

Maybe it had been when he'd returned from college? Shortly beforehand, Conner had returned home. Since Riley was married and out of the house, it had been the four of them and the place had felt a little crowded since then.

Now that Conner was out, he still felt as if he was a stranger in his parents' home. He was cautious when he came in, afraid that he'd catch his parents together since they'd obviously gotten used to having the home to themselves.

As he snuck in the back door, making sure to not wake his mother, he glanced around his childhood home.

In the past few years, his mother had redecorated each room. Almost every piece of furniture in the home was new, making the home feel even more foreign.

Climbing the stairs to his bedroom, he realized that even that had changed. After he'd moved to college, his mother had changed his bedroom into a guest room since it was the closest to the stairs and had easiest access to the bathroom across the hallway.

Now, as he lay in bed trying to shut down from the long day, he realized it was time for him to venture out on his own. After all, he had secured the perfect job for his future thanks to his uncle Todd.

It was high time he secured the rest of his life as well.

Bright and early the next morning, he swung by Sara's Nook for some pastries and coffee before heading to the job site. He figured he'd have to butter Rose up in order to convince her of his next move.

It wasn't that she had anything against him purchasing

his own place in Hidden Cove. It was that he was going to have to swallow his pride and agree to live in a house she'd designed.

After all, over the past few months, he'd been teasing her about her house plans. Sure, he wanted to make a few changes of his own, but the fact was, she was more talented than he liked to let on.

He set down an entire box of her favorite sprinkle-covered donuts and a large coffee the way she liked it, with a spoonful of caramel sauce, and waited for her to arrive.

Five minutes later, when she walked in, he was all smiles.

"Morning," he said cheerfully.

"Morning," she almost groaned.

He could tell by her disheveled appearance that she had not gotten a good night sleep. Her long dark hair was in a braid that fell over her shoulder. She was wearing a cotton hat and scarf to ward off the chill in the air that morning. When she removed her heavy coat, he could see the grey sweater and jeans she was wearing underneath.

Her attire, along with the work boots, and the lack of makeup didn't hinder her beauty.

"What's all this?" she asked, eyeing the box of sweets and the coffee cup he held up for her.

"A peace offering," he said easily.

"For?" She took the cup from him and waited.

He shrugged. "Do I have to have a reason to buy my employee..."—her eyes narrowed and he coughed slightly before correcting himself—"coworker breakfast?"

"What do you want?" she asked after opening the box and seeing the Halloween-decorated donuts. She sat on the edge of his desk and crossed her arms over her chest.

"Who? Me?" He tried to act innocent but failed miserably.

"I am in no mood for games today," she warned. "I had a flat tire this morning and had to change it. Now I'll have to head into town on my lunch break and—"

"Why didn't you call me?" he interrupted, causing her eyes to narrow even more.

"Because," she said slowly, "I am more than capable of changing a tire on my own."

"Of course, you are." He acted slightly shocked. "But on a truck that size, it could be dangerous. Even I wouldn't change a flat on my truck alone." He shook his head. It was true, with the large tires on her truck, he would have called his brother to give him a hand. Besides, it would have taken half the time to change it with help.

She looked a little deflated at that information. "I didn't think of it," she said with a shrug as she pulled a donut from the box. "So, what's the real reason you brought me donuts?"

He figured she really wasn't in the mood to mess around and decided the best course of action was the direct route.

"I talked to my uncle this morning, and he's agreed to set one of the lots aside for me," he said quickly before reaching for a donut for himself.

He'd expected her to be surprised, but instead, she looked at him through narrowed eyelids.

"You're purchasing a home in Hidden Cove?" she asked slowly.

"Yes," he said with a smile.

"Why?" she surprised him by asking.

"Because, well, it's time I got out of my parents' place. And since my brother and cousins will be close by"—he shrugged—"I guess I'm hoping to recreate what my parents and aunts and uncles have on Beachview."

"A family street?" she asked him.

"Yeah." He felt slightly relieved that she understood.

"So you'll probably want one of the lots with the ocean view?" she asked him.

"I've picked out lot five. Right next to the Jenkins's place."

The home they were building for Aiden and Suzie was just across the street. Technically, it wasn't officially in Hidden Cove but on some land of its own just to the south of the lowest lots that backed the view.

"So..." Her smile started slowly. "You're going to build and live in one of my floor plans? Are you sure you will feel comfortable living in—how did you describe it?—a jumbled floor plan filled with cabobbled disarray and anti-feng-shui?"

He winced as she threw his words back at him.

"Not all of your floor plans are..." Her eyebrows shot up, waiting for his next words. "Chaotic," he finished with a smile.

Instead of arguing, she rubbed the bridge of her nose and sighed heavily.

"Which plan were you thinking?" she finally asked.

For the next two hours, in between his normal work schedule, he tried to pick out all the options for his very own future home.

For some reason, the more riled up Rose was, the more fun he had. She grew angry at him when he picked out something she didn't think should go in the home.

Each time he pointed out that it would be his home, she'd reply that she would, along with his family, have to visit him in it.

"If I'm so bad at this, why don't you just pick out all the options yourself," he said, standing up. He wasn't frustrated at her, more at the process. He didn't know what would look good in a home. All that mattered to him was that he had a place of his own. "I've got work to do," he said, before rushing out of the trailer.

He had stormed halfway across the gravel parking lot before realizing that he'd left without his coat or gloves. Turning back around, he stepped back inside and found Rose huddled at the computer, tears rolling down her cheeks.

The sight of her crying broke him. He rushed over to her, gathered her in his arms, and held onto her while she tried to excuse her tears away.

"I'm just tired," she said into his shoulder.

"I was an ass," he said softly.

"You were, but this has nothing to do with—"

"Shh," he stopped her. "I know when I've caused someone pain. For that I'm sorry." He sighed. "I'm not frustrated at you. It's just... well, I don't know what it is I want in a home yet. I find this entire process... daunting," he admitted. "I let it get me agitated, and I took it out on you." He lifted her chin with a finger until her tear-filled eyes met his. "For that, I'm so very sorry." He lowered his face to gently lay his lips over hers. "Honest, you'd be helping me out if you just picked everything to go in the home." He slowly smiled. "That way if I don't like it, I can always blame you."

She chuckled and wiped her eyes dry. "Go, do your work. I'll finish this for you," she finally said as she stepped away from him. "I didn't mean to lose it," she said as he headed towards the door.

Instead of replying, he nodded, then stopped, picked up

the box of donuts, and set them on the edge of her desk, where she grabbed one up. Then he took another one before putting on his coat and gloves and heading back outside.

Whatever he did now, he knew he had to prove to Rose that he could be something beyond the big brother role he'd fallen into. Actually, he didn't know what Rose thought of him or if she did like him like his brother had mentioned.

He was getting mixed signals on the kisses. The first one had been a dud, but the rest, the way she'd reacted to the other kisses, had him tossing and turning all night long and dreaming of holding her again.

Damn. He was in trouble. H needed to clear his mind, so he turned and headed towards what would soon be his very first home.

CHAPTER FIVE

Designing Jacob's home should have been easy for her to do. After all, when she'd picked all the options with Blake a few months back, she'd automatically known her favorite choices.

She continued to berate herself for allowing him to get to her. Actually, her tears hadn't really been about him earlier. She was just having one of those days. Finding the flat tire on her truck had just been the icing to top everything off that morning.

The lack of sleep the night before had been partially his fault. The rest of the blame landed solely on her when she'd decided to have a glass of wine and sit in the hot tub on the back deck after Jacob had dropped her off. The hot tub had done its job and relaxed her while the wine had caused her mind to wander and imagine what it would be like to actually be with Jacob.

This, of course, had led to a disappointing night's sleep filled with images of Jacob and her entangled in passion-filled wonder.

She'd slept through her first alarm and after a quick,

very cold shower, due to the pilot light being out on her water heater, she'd quickly dressed and left. But then she'd had to re-dress after the very muddy event of changing her truck's tire.

Now, as she tried to focus on the task at hand and imagined Jacob living day to day in the four-bedroom house, she couldn't envision him enjoying the soft pastel beach colors that she would choose. So, instead, she chose a neutral soft cream for the walls, a dark rich hickory for the wood flooring, slate blue cabinets in all the bathrooms with steel grey cabinets everywhere else, and accessories for an almost farmhouse feeling for the rest of the home.

She opted to add a wood stove fireplace to the living room and a stone hearth fireplace in the main bedroom. She could just imagine Jacob enjoying them both on cold nights. Of course, the minor changes would mean that the plans would have to be sent off to the structural engineering firm that reviewed and stamped the plans with their seal for county approval.

Since they'd have to do that anyway, she tweaked the plan a little more by adding an additional sink in the laundry room and garage. She even added an outdoor shower along the back of the house so anyone coming up from the beach could rinse off before stepping into the mud room.

By the time she heard Jacob come back into the trailer, she had every option picked out for his new home and had sent the revised plans off to the engineering firm for approval.

She stepped out of her small office, and he glanced up from his computer when she set his folder in front of him.

"Your options." She scooted the folder towards him.

"Go over them and if you want anything changed... you know where to find me." She turned to go.

"Rose." Hearing the low tone of his voice made her stop and turn back towards him. When her eyes met his, he smiled slightly, and she felt her heart skip in her chest. "Thank you."

Feeling tired and worn down, she nodded before returning to her office without saying anything further to him.

Half an hour later, he knocked on her opened office door and leaned against the door jamb, his arms crossed over his chest casually.

"I like the changes you made to the floorplan," he said easily, his eyes scanning her face. There was an inkling of concern in his eyes, and he was no doubt looking for any hint of her emotions.

She waited, unsure what to say to him as he continued to scan her eyes. She watched him shift slightly and move over to sit in the chair across from her desk.

"The color schemes are nice too." He motioned to the samples that filled the other half of her office.

It was one of the reasons Jacob's desk was out in the front room. That and her insistence that she would need the privacy of the room to meet with potential buyers. It had been the first time she could remember winning an argument with Jacob.

Then again, most of their disagreements over the years had been about trivial things, such as who would be captain in a game of capture the flag or whether a play was out or in when they'd been playing beach volleyball.

In the last few weeks, she'd seen such a change in Jacob. Not only in his attitude, but in the way that he treated her.

For the first time in her life, he was going out of his way to be extra kind to her.

The passion with which he'd kissed her last night was a sure sign that more than just his feelings for her had changed. There was no denying his desire or hers.

She may have been able to hide the way she felt about him for years, but now that he had let that genie out of the bottle, the question was, what was he going to do now? Would he use that knowledge against her? Tease her? Taunt her with it?

She didn't know if she could trust him with her heart. Not that he was a vicious person. On the contrary, as an adult, she could look back at everything Jacob had done as a sort of childish flirting.

Then again, he'd treated most of his cousins and family members the same way. Which is why, growing up, she'd always assumed he'd thought of her as a sister.

"Anything can be changed, if you want," she suggested. She reached over and took the file from him and opened it up to show him the images of the floor plan. "For example, the fireplace location." She pointed to the area.

"It's fine," he broke in. "Perfect actually. Right there close enough to the backdoor for bringing in firewood and still good enough to heat the whole house."

She narrowed her eyes at him. "Okay," she said slowly. "What about the color schemes?" She motioned to the wall behind him. "If you want..."

"I like the blue and grey cabinets. The walls"—he shrugged slightly—"don't really matter. They will need repainting over the years anyway. The colors are easy enough to change if I don't like it."

She held in a chuckle but apparently not good enough because his eyebrows shot up.

"What?" he asked.

She shook her head. "It's... nothing."

He smiled slightly. "No, go ahead. What?"

"You are your mother's son. If I remember correctly, she's painted the walls in her art studio more than a dozen times because she liked changing things up," she finally said.

He smiled and she felt her breath catch. God, he looked so damn good when he smiled. She had to admit it to herself that she was falling even more in love with him than she'd been all her life. If that was even possible.

"Yeah, I guess one thing I've learned over the years of growing up under the same roof as a famous painter is that what's more important than the color of the walls is what art you have hanging on them."

She couldn't help but smile back at him. "Once your plans get back from the engineers, you can start the work on getting approval from the city and county."

He nodded and stood to go, then stopped. "How about we grab some lunch?"

She frowned. "I needed my lunch break to drop the truck off to get the tire patched."

He tilted his head slightly as if he was thinking. "I'll follow you into town and while they're working on the tire, we can head to Baked and grab a pizza?"

She nodded quickly. "Sure," she said. She hadn't wanted to sit at the tire store alone and go without lunch while they worked on her tire. Grabbing her coat and purse, she followed Jacob outside only to come up short when his phone rang.

She stood on the little deck to the trailer as he talked. She assumed it was his brother.

"Kara's awake and alert," Jacob said after he hung up.

"And, apparently, engaged to my brother." He rolled his eyes and chuckled. "Anyone was around yesterday knew that it wouldn't be long before he popped the question. It was obvious he's totally gone for her."

"That's good news." She followed him out to where their trucks were parked. "Any word yet on who shot her?"

His smile slipped. "A guy by the name of Kurt Collins." He shrugged. "There's a statewide search out for the guy and his blue truck. No word yet on if they've caught him or why he shot at Kara. Robin, Kara's sister, mentioned that Thomas Carson had been snooping around her property a few times."

"It just doesn't make sense. I mean"—she glanced around—"this property is pretty amazing, and I get the potential for income it has, but to kill over it?" She shook her head. "I don't see it."

"Yeah." Jacob ran his hands through his hair. "Because of the shooting, Conner says that my uncle is hiring security for around here." He motioned to the small construction trailer. "We're supposed to meet them here around one."

"Do you think..." She stopped as her own heart raced. "You don't think they'll come back around here, do you?"

He shrugged. "I doubt it, but we're not going to take any chances. Besides, now that we've officially started selling homes, we need to keep the onlookers off the property for insurance purposes anyway."

"Right." She relaxed slightly.

"I'll follow you into town." He motioned towards her truck.

Driving into town, she couldn't get what had happened to Kara out of her mind. She'd driven by the place where she'd been shot yesterday morning. There was a makeshift shrine of flowers set up in the spot now.

She figured she'd swing by Suzie's flower shop, All in Bloom, and grab some flowers to deliver to the hospital herself.

After all, Kara had been so nice to chat with. Possibly even a potential close friend. If she was going to be living in Pride for the next few years while they finished out the subdivision, she needed friends to help bide the time and keep her sane.

Especially if she was going to be successful in not exposing the feelings she had for Jacob any further. She doubted she could hold out for too long. Especially with how Jacob was treating her and being so attentive. It was as if he was a completely different person lately. Did that mean he really did have strong feelings for her? Something that went beyond friendship? That possibility had her questioning his motives the entire time she sat across from him at the pizzeria.

"You're quiet," he pointed out after their pizza was delivered.

"Thoughtful," she corrected.

"Okay, what is it you're thinking about?" he asked after taking a slice of pizza.

Even the fact that they both had the same favorite pizza ran through her head. After all, most guys didn't like mushroom and onion pizza, but she remembered that he'd always liked the same toppings as she did.

"Kara," she said with a shrug. "I'm thinking of stopping off and getting some flowers and delivering them up to her after work."

"She'd like that. We filled her room with half of Suzie's flower shop last night before I left. It helps to have a florist who owns her own shop in the family," he joked.

"Right." She chuckled.

"I was going to head up that way myself, if you want to ride together?" he offered.

She thought about it for a moment and after replaying how the last time she'd ridden with him had ended, shook her head.

"No, thank you. I wouldn't want to put you out. Besides, I need to run a few errands in Edgeview anyway," she lied.

His eyebrows shot up slightly, but then he shrugged. "If you change your mind..."

"Thanks," she said, and she finished her pizza.

Living in a small town for the past few months, she had grown to realize just how nice it was to know people where you lived. When you were lonely, it only took a trip to the grocery store or the library or pizza shop to bump into someone and strike up a conversation.

Now, however, it appeared that the entire town noticed Jacob and her sitting there having lunch together. It wasn't their first lunch as coworkers, but it was the first since he'd kissed her, and she'd kissed him back.

Which of course, in her mind at least, gave more meaning to all of the looks people were giving them. She tried to brush it off as her imagination.

When Jacob drove her back to the tire store, she was informed that it hadn't just been her tire that had been damaged. Whatever she'd hit had caused her rim to be bent as well and they wouldn't have a new one until tomorrow. Since she didn't want to continue driving on the small spare, she told them to keep the truck until it was fixed.

"Looks like I'll be driving you tonight anyway," Jacob joked as they walked back out of the tire store.

She wanted to tell him not to worry about it, that she'd just wait until tomorrow to head to Edgeview and deliver flowers to Kara, but he added, "You know, so you can run those errands."

Right. She'd lied about needing to get some things done in town.

"Thanks," she added, figuring she could come up with something she needed to do before the end of work.

After all, if she changed her plans suddenly, Jacob would know she had lied earlier. The last time Jacob had caught her in a lie, she hadn't lived it down for more than five years.

And yet, somehow, that memory made her smile for the rest of the workday.

CHAPTER SIX

He knew that Rose had lied to him about needing to run errands in town, and he questioned why. Why hadn't she wanted to ride into town with him? Was she trying to avoid him? Had he ruined their friendship with that kiss last night?

She'd seemed to enjoy it, but he knew she'd been angry the other night when she'd stormed out of the truck. He'd convinced himself that it was for the best.

This lie wasn't like the last time he'd caught her lying. She'd been twelve or thirteen and had fibbed about having a boyfriend, whom she couldn't even provide a name for. So he'd done what any pubescent teenage boy would have done. He'd teased her for as long as he could. A few years later, his father had found out and smacked him on the back of the head as a warning.

That was the year he'd realized the feelings he'd been having for Rose went beyond anything he'd ever felt for anyone before.

Sitting in the same truck with her for the twenty-minute

drive through the falling snow, he tried to make the conversation as light as he could.

He asked her about her parents. He knew that Ric Derby had more than a half a dozen high-end art galleries across the States, most of which included some of his mother's paintings.

Her mother, Roberta, or Rob, as everyone called her, was head of security for all of the galleries, a full-time job that she had gained when she'd retired as a detective. He now understood that had happened after she'd been shot.

"So that's when my cousins Camilla and Cora decided that their new brother Liam really belonged to the circus," she said with a chuckle.

"Okay, so their father is your father's brother?" he asked, trying to get her family's dynamics down.

"No. Ethan Knight, my uncle, is my mother's half-brother." She shifted slightly. "That's a fun story in and of itself. My dad has a half-sister, Katie, who has a full brother, Dante, who lives in Italy." She glanced over at him. "Too long of a story for this trip. But shortly after she was born, my mother was stolen by her father, who was a thief."

He glanced over at her. "A..."

She smiled. "Yup, a thief. He raised her until he up and died, leaving her to live on the streets of Portland. Then, shortly after her eighteenth birthday, when the gang she was in was gunned down in front of her—she was the only survivor and witness—she was taken in by one of the policemen who found the killers. A few years later, after becoming a detective herself, she took on my father's case."

"Wait, how did she ever find out about your uncle?" he asked. "I have more questions, but that one is first."

She chuckled and shifted the bundle of flowers she'd picked out for Kara. "She didn't. Ethan found her when he spotted her at a hospital and recognized her instantly. It appears he'd been looking for her his entire life. So he broke into her apartment and left this." She reached up and touched the extremely old medallion pendant hanging around her neck.

"It looks old," he said, not wanting to take his eyes off the road for too long since the snow was coming down much faster now.

"It's supposedly from Brazil, 1600s." She smiled and lowered her voice. "If you believe in legends, it's rumored to be a piece from El Dorado." She wiggled her eyebrows at him.

"But it's not gold," he pointed out.

"Exactly." She pointed at him as if that explained something and laughed.

"And so, you just wear it around your neck?"

She looked down at it and nodded. "It's the last thing my mother has of her childhood. She claims it is the reason she found her family and that someday"—she looked out into the dark snowy night—"it will help me find something very important too."

He was silent. "So I guess insanity runs in your family too," he joked after a moment and then enjoyed the sound of her laughter. "Did I ever tell you that my father claims to have seen the ghost of my grandfather? Oh, and a few years back, my entire family saw a ghost family in Matthew and Blake's house."

She chuckled. "Blake has told me the tragic story of the family that used to live in their house. How someone had murdered the mother and stolen the little girl and then, shortly after, the father committed suicide because he was under investigation for his wife and daughter's murder. The murderer went on to raise the girl on her own. The story was eerily similar to my mother's own story." She turned towards him. "Did you really see them? The ghosts?"

He shrugged. "I think Matt slipped something in the eggnog," he joked. "I don't know what I saw, but the rest of my family brings it up every Christmas and speculates even further." He'd been in complete denial about seeing the apparition since the moment the fuzzy images had appeared in front of everyone that night.

She smiled. "Sounds like a good time."

He laughed as he pulled into the hospital parking lot. "It is."

The visit with Kara and Conner went smoother than he'd imagined. Kara looked pale but happy with his brother sitting beside her on the bed. Rose chatted with Kara as if they were old friends, and she even got Kara to laugh and joke when she told the story of how Conner and he had spent one entire summer chasing her around with sea slugs.

He'd forgotten that and had to laugh himself until she'd mentioned that she'd been mentally distraught enough to go crying to her father about the whole ordeal.

He realized that he'd been nothing but a bully and started questioning how she'd put up with him all these years. And how was she supposed to forgive him for all the terrible tricks he'd played on her? Could he ever make it up to her?

"How about we grab some dinner?" he asked as they walked out of the hospital. The snow was still falling and at this point there was almost half a foot on the ground, which he knew would make the drive back to Pride slow.

"Sure," she said, buttoning her coat up all the way and slipping on her hat before they stepped outside together.

"They're a cute couple," she said after he started driving to one of his favorite restaurants in town.

"Yeah." He nodded. "It's funny to see Conner so happy."

"Why funny?"

He shrugged. "For the past few years, he's been..." He tried to think of the proper word. "Indecisive."

"About?"

"Everything. I think he only joined the Coast Guard because he had nothing else to do."

"But he's good at it. He was part of the crew that rescued the group whose helicopter went down a while back, right?" she asked.

"Yeah." He smiled and felt pride flood him when he remembered how his brother had saved the four-person crew. "He's good at it and something tells me he's not planning on leaving it anytime soon. Actually, Allen Masters has hinted about giving him a more permanent teaching position."

"That's great," she said as he shut off the truck. She turned to the restaurant. "I love this place." She smiled. "They have the best sweet potato fries here."

"My favorite," he said with a chuckle. "But don't you dare tell my dad I said that."

He hadn't planned on dinner being anything more than a quick stop for food, but almost two hours later, they strolled out of the restaurant, laughing together.

"I can't believe I actually did that to you," he said, shaking his head as he opened the passenger door for her. He stopped her from getting into the truck by touching her elbow. "If I haven't said it before, I'm sorry. I'm sorry for all of the terrible things I did when I was a skinned-knee, snot-nosed boy," he said with a grin, using the words she'd used to describe him and his brother many times.

Her smile caused him to relax some. Then she reached

up and ran her hand over his scruffy face, and he realized it had been a few days since he'd shaved.

"I like the beard," she said, as if she'd read his mind. "I guess you no longer have skinned knees or a snotty nose." Her hand remained on his face.

"No," he agreed with her. "And you're not the skinny awkward girl you used to be. I do miss seeing those cute little braids you used to wear in your hair," he said softly, reaching up and running his fingers through her long curly hair as they inched closer together.

Within a breath away from her, he waited until she closed the distance, wanting her to make the move this time so that he understood that she wanted him as much as he wanted her.

When her lips brushed against his, his fingers closed in her hair and softly held her as his entire body heated. When he felt her soft breasts bump against his chest, he held in a groan as he pulled back.

"Come on, lets head out and get those errands of yours done before the snow gets too deep," he said, helping her into the truck. When he got behind the wheel and started warming up the truck, he turned to her and asked. "Where to?"

She was quiet and seemed to think for a while.

"Home. I can run my errands later this weekend." She added, "I don't want us to get trapped in this storm."

He tried not to smile at her and focused instead on backing out of the parking lot.

"Don't give me that look," she warned him as he started heading home.

"What look?" He faked shock.

She narrowed her eyes at him. "Jacob, I've known you my entire life, and I know the look you make when you gloat." She pointed a finger at him. "That, right there, is your gloaty face."

He chuckled. "Gloaty?"

"It's a real word. Look it up." She crossed her arms over her chest and pouted, causing his smile to grow.

"Okay, I believe you." He focused on the road.

They fell into silence as he concentrated on driving safely out of town. When the busy lights of the town disappeared, replaced by long stretches of dark road, he relaxed again. The sound of the windshield wipers broke the silence with their soft scraping sounds. The snowflakes in his headlights seemed to grow bigger the closer they got to Pride.

"I hear it's supposed to let up soon," Rose said softly.

"Yeah, soon. We're supposed to pour the basements on my brother's lot and the Jenkins' lot this week," he added, not taking his eyes from the road.

"Thank you for driving," she said when the new brightly lit 'You are now entering Pride' sign came into view. "I wouldn't have wanted to drive in this alone."

"Any time," he added as he turned off the main highway and headed towards her place.

"They should have my truck ready for me tomorrow around noon." She sighed.

He chanced a glance at her. "Want me to pick you up for work?" he asked as he pulled into her long driveway.

She waited until he parked in front of the garage, the bright floodlights of the house showcasing the fresh snow in the yard and piled up on the deck and stairs.

"No," she finally answered as she removed her seatbelt. "What I want is for you to come inside," she said softly.

His heart skipped, and then his dick jumped at the thought of being with Rose. Finally.

She moved across the space, then with her eyes locked

on his, slowly climbed onto his lap. She buried her hands in his hair, and he heard her breath hitch.

"Come inside, be with me?" she asked.

"If things don't go..." he started, unable to finish the thought of possibly losing her if things turned bad between them.

"Even if this doesn't work"—she motioned between them—"nothing will change between us."

"If I believed that..."

She stopped him by leaning in and kissing him, deeply, fully, until he believed her with every fiber of his being.

His hands moved to her hips, forcing her to move over him, grinding against him as her hands moved over his shoulders, trying to push his coat off his shoulders.

His hands moved up, exposing the skin under her sweater, and he felt her shiver when the cold of the night hit her.

He'd shut off the truck earlier and now it was as cold in the truck as it was outside.

Without thinking, he yanked open his door and lifted her in his arms to carry her inside.

"My purse." She laughed and stopped him before he could shut the door. "And your keys." She motioned to the truck.

"Damn." He'd almost forgotten everything.

He didn't want to let her go, so he shifted her in his arms, reached back into the truck, and grabbed her purse, his keys, and his wallet, which held his one and only condom.

Shutting the truck door with his foot, he started up the snow-covered walkway towards the house while she hunted through her purse for her keys.

The moment they stepped into the house, her lips were

back on his. He nudged the front door shut behind them as she dumped her purse on the table by the door.

"Where's your room?" he asked.

"Up the stairs, third door on the right," she answered a little breathlessly as she tugged to free him from his coat. She tossed her own on the floor at the top of the stairs.

By the time he stepped into her room, she'd removed both of their coats, which had caused them both to be a little breathless.

CHAPTER SEVEN

Rose didn't want to stop and think about what she was doing. If it was the best choice, if what she was demanding from Jacob, wanting from him, was good for her at this time in her life. If she allowed herself enough time to think about it, she'd convince herself to stop and to turn him out into the snowy night.

But her body and heart wanted, and at the moment, she was willing to chance everything. Anything, really, to be with him. Even if it was just for this one night. After all, how long had she wanted this? Wanted him?

He loosened his hold on her and her body slid slowly down his, making her vibrate with want even more. When her feet finally touched the ground, she realized that both of their work boots were still on and would most likely take more time to remove that she wanted to spend at the moment.

She was thankful when he continued kissing her, making her forget everything except him. Then, as he started backing her up towards her bed, he pulled away.

"Here," he said, taking her hands and guiding her to sit down, "let me get your boots off."

She sat down on the edge of the bed and watched his dark head as he bent over her while he slowly untied her work boots. Her breathing became more labored the closer that he got to removing them.

When he had removed her boots, he quickly untied and removed his own and then set both pairs at the end of the bed.

When he came back to her, he took her hands in his and pulled her up to stand next to him. His hands went to her hips as she wrapped her arms around his shoulders, and then he bent his head to kiss her again.

Her entire body swayed as he took the kiss deeper, causing her desire for him to double. Needing to see more of him, to feel more of his skin against hers, she started tugging his shirt over his head. When she tossed it on the ground, she leaned back to take a moment to appreciate just how amazing he was.

His toned muscles flexed under her gaze and called for her to explore and appreciate every cord with her hands. Her fingers slid slowly over him while her eyes followed along the same path, and his breath hitched.

When she reached the clasp of his jeans, his hands moved to cover hers.

"Rose." A soft groan vibrated his chest, and she felt a desire to run her lips against his skin. "I need a moment," he finished saying.

Smiling, her eyes locked with his. "You've had a life-time." Then she leaned in and covered his flat nipple with her lips.

His hands buried in her hair, holding her to the spot as

she ran her tongue over him, causing his nipple to pucker for her.

"Rose." This time his tone was a warning.

She glanced up at him and smiled. "Yes?"

"You're on very dangerous ground," he warned, but seeing his smile, she continued as her nails scraped down his back.

She arched into his hands as they roamed up under her sweater. Feeling his fingers on her skin had soft moans escaping her own lips. She allowed him to remove her sweater and the light camisole she wore underneath. Standing in front of him in her jeans and bra, she reached for the clasp of his jeans only to have his hands cover hers again.

"Let's... take a moment," he said, cupping her face in his hands. "Like you said, we've had a lifetime, what's a little longer?" He kissed her and even though she felt the desire for speed, she allowed him to go slower and savored the kiss.

When his hands roamed up and cupped her breasts, his name escaped her lips.

She should have known that being with him like this, having him touch her, kiss her, would be powerful. Hadn't she spent a lifetime dreaming about moments like this? Now that it was here, all she could think of was her desire for him to hurry, to reach that glorious end with him.

"Jacob, please," she begged, trying once again to pull him towards the bed.

"Let me," he said, walking her backwards to the edge of the bed.

Instead of laying her down, he reached for the clasp of her jeans. With his eyes locked on hers, he slid her jeans down her hips until they pooled on the floor at her feet.

When she stepped out of them, his eyes moved over her

entire body, and she watched his desire clearly heat his gaze.

Then his hands were on her bare skin, and she shivered at the excitement of him touching her. She felt as if she was floating, the feeling of his hands and his mouth the only thing rooting her in place.

When she felt her back on the mattress, a chuckle escaped her. She didn't know why she found it funny, but figured it was just the finality of feeling his weight pinning her down.

"What's so funny?" he asked as his mouth trailed down her neck, and goose bumps formed all over her body.

"You. Me. Here. Like this," she said with a sigh. "Finally," she added when he glanced down at her. His smile caused her heart to jump in her chest.

Pulling him back down to her lips, she marveled at the taste of him. She wrapped her legs around him and held on, silently willing him to take what he wanted from her.

His fingers dipped below her panties and she stilled, anticipating feeling his skin brushing against her sensitive desire. She jumped slightly as his finger brushed and then dipped into her, and her arms tightened around his shoulders as her eyes closed.

"That's it, hold onto me," he said in a low tone. "I've got you, baby." He started to move slowly in and out of her slickness. "My god, you feel so good."

"Jacob, I... can't." She bit her bottom lip.

"Let go," he begged. "Please," he said against her lips. "God, I really want to feel you let go."

When he covered her nipple with his mouth, she felt her entire body jolt and release, as if he'd willed it of her. As if he'd been in control of her all along.

For the next few moments, she was floating, blissfully

unaware of anything beyond her body's aftermath of pure unhindered sexual release.

She hadn't realized he'd removed the rest of his clothes and only vaguely heard him opening a condom package before she felt him sliding up her body. Smiling, she wrapped her legs around his and this time knew that he wouldn't hold back.

When he slid into her, she enjoyed the sound of his deep moan before he laid his lips over hers again.

"I've wanted this, wanted you, for as long as I can remember," he said between kisses.

The amount of passion vibrating from him assured her that his words were true.

"Me too." She sighed as she gripped him, trying to hold on while she felt her entire body building once again.

How did he have such control over her? She'd never imagined being so overwhelmed with desire that she was unable to hold back or wait. Feeling a wave of release wash over her again, she dug her nails softly into his shoulders and cried out.

"My god," she heard him say against her skin.

She wanted him to experience the amount of desire that she was feeling and wrapped her legs around his hips, moving with him as she poured everything she had ever felt for him into her kiss.

She hadn't expected that by doing so she would once again build up her own desires and when she felt him tense above her, she too was once again falling into the abyss.

Sleeping with Jacob beside her reminded her of a few things. One, her bed was way too small for someone of his stature, and two, she regretted the fact that when he awoke in the morning, he would be greeted with her hot pink sheets and comforter.

Actually, her entire room was still decorated in the hot pink items she'd chosen when she'd been sixteen, including a few posters on her walls of teenage bands or movie stars that she used to have crushes on.

"I can hear you thinking, you know," Jacob said with a chuckle.

"No, you can't." She moaned as he shifted to tuck her into his arms.

He sighed as he rested his face in her hair. "God, you smell good."

She smiled and leaned further against his chest. "Just don't judge me when you wake up and see how pink my room is in the morning."

He was silent for a while, and when she looked up at him, she could tell he was trying to see it in the darkness of the night.

"How pink?" he asked.

"Very." She moaned and buried her face in his chest.

She felt and heard him chuckle again. "No guarantees. After all, I do live for teasing you. Remember?"

How many times over the years had she accused him of just that? It had seemed true all those years of her childhood with him, right there, teasing and what she used to deem torturing her. Now, however, things were... different.

"I guess this changes everything between us," she said with a sigh.

Again, he chuckled. "You think?" His arm wrapped around her, and he ran his fingers over her skin softly, making her realize she was even more tired than she'd thought.

"Just don't... judge me for my room. I was sixteen the last time I painted and decorated it," she said with a sigh.

"You should see my room." He groaned softly.

"Oh?" She glanced up at him through the darkness. "Is it the same as when you were a kid?" she asked.

"No." He glanced down at her. "My mother redecorated it the year I left for college. Now I'm sleeping in a room that is better suited for guests. Lacy doilies, quilted blankets, and all."

She smiled. "I bet you fit right in."

He started running his hands through her hair, and she practically purred and arched into his touch.

"I'll wager I fit in a pink room much better," he replied.

She smiled and felt her heart skip at the thought of him staying there with her.

"You're welcome to stay as long as you want," she said between yawns.

"I might just take you up on that offer," he said before she drifted off.

First thing the next morning, just as the sunlight was starting to light up her room, she heard him gasp.

"You weren't joking. Do you think there is enough pink in this room?" he asked.

She rolled over and noticed him standing naked on the massive bright pink rug that covered the hardwood floor just outside her bathroom door.

"Ugh," she moaned, covering her face with her blankets. "I did warn you."

"Yeah, but..." She heard him chuckle. "It's hot pink and everywhere. It's like someone threw up after downing a case of Pepto Bismol."

"Just... go away." She groaned, trying not to laugh at his joke. It was true, though. As an adult, she could see why her parents had tried to talk her out of the bright color. But she'd had her mind set on it back then.

"Hey," she heard him say after he'd stepped into the bathroom, "at least the bathroom isn't pink."

She listened to him turn on the shower and decided after a few moments that it was safe to uncover her face from the blanket. She screamed when his face was inches from hers as he smiled down at her.

"Come on," he said, tossing the blanket off her, exposing her to the cold of the room. She immediately tried to cover up, but he hoisted her up in his arms. "It's shower time."

There was no use arguing with him, since he had a firm hold on her. Besides, she knew that she probably had less than half an hour before her own alarm would go off.

When he stepped into the shower, holding her in his arms, she smiled and wrapped her arms around his neck.

"Think our boss will be upset at us if we're a little late to work this morning?" she practically purred.

"I doubt he'll even notice." His smile grew. "Since he's right here in the shower with you."

She reached up and punched him lightly on the shoulder. "Just for that, you get to wash my back." She turned her back on him and tossed a washcloth in his direction.

His arms wrapped around her waist as he pulled her back against his chest.

"Just as long as I can wash the rest of you as well," he said softly as his hand moved over her.

When his lips gently glided over her shoulder, her knees buckled and she melted against his chest. It dawned on her that, at that moment, she would have given him anything.

CHAPTER EIGHT

The following weeks went by quickly. Halloween came and went in the small town and ghosts and ghouls were replaced with holiday decorations.

There was the standard Jordan Thanksgiving family dinner, where the entire clan got together at the closed Golden Oar restaurant for a massive meal. Rose's parents even came down and joined in the fun, and since he'd taken Rose up on her offer for him to move in with her, it meant a few days back at home while her parents were in town.

They were both really enjoying each other's company at night, but he figured a few days apart from each other wouldn't hurt.

They hadn't told any of his family yet, and he was guessing by the way she acted around everyone that she didn't want anyone to know about them.

At least not yet. At this point, he would do anything and everything to keep returning to her place each night.

When his mother had asked him where he was sleeping at night, he'd mentioned that he was housesitting for a friend. Jacob was pretty sure that his mother knew exactly where he was and what he was doing. He was just thankful his mother didn't investigate any further. She had, however, given him a look that had assured him that the conversation wasn't over.

Shortly after Kara's shooting, his brother had called and asked him to pick up a gift for Kara's homecoming from the hospital and deliver it to their apartment. So, he'd driven up to Carrie's Sanctuary just outside of town and picked up a small black puppy that Conner had arranged to adopt.

It hit him a little hard knowing that his brother was moving on and starting his future life with Kara. He really liked Kara and her sister Robin and was happy that Kara would soon be part of the family.

The problem was it got him thinking about his own future. One that, in his mind at least, had always potentially included Rose.

When he'd been leaving the animal sanctuary that day last month, he had noticed an older yellow Lab mix nursing her brand-new litter of puppies in Carrie's office.

"That's Sophie," Carrie had said with a smile. "She came to us just in time to give birth to twelve little ones."

"These little ones are fresh from the oven," he'd joked since all the puppies looked like little tan loaves of bread. "Actually, they look like they haven't been fully cooked yet." He laughed.

He'd walked over to kneel by the new family and had fallen head over heels with one of the small yellow and white babies and was thinking about taking one of them home himself. But then something strange happened. He spent more time with Sophie instead of the puppies and soon the new mother had melted his heart.

"What happens to her when all her babies have been adopted?" he'd asked.

Carrie shrugged. "We'll try and find her a good home."

"How long will it be before she can find a home?" he asked as the dog laid her head in his lap and looked up at him with big sad chocolate eyes.

"Well, we'll be able to start adopting out the babies at nine weeks. Sometimes it can take a while though. I'd say mama here will be ready to go to her forever home in about twelve weeks."

"Perfect," he said, trying to convince himself that it was enough time to get Rose comfortable with the idea of a dog around her place. He knew from experience that she liked dogs since there had always been dogs around all of the Jordan households.

He remembered that her parents had had a small terrier of sorts when Rose had been younger, so he doubted she'd have too much of a problem with the idea of the dog. But since he was staying at her place most nights, he had to officially run the idea of letting Sophie stay there by Rose.

For the first time since he'd returned home from college, he actually looked forward to heading home from work each night. The first few nights together, Rose and he had grabbed dinner on the way home, then things had been all heat and speed once they stepped inside the house.

Last night, almost a week after her parents had returned to Portland after their short Thanksgiving trip, had been one of the first nights he and Rose had cooked at the house instead of going out. He'd helped her make spaghetti in the large kitchen and realized how thankful he was to be back with her during the nights.

After dinner, they had sat on the back deck, huddled together around the firepit that was tucked with the hot tub under the cover of the deck and listened to the rain falling around them.

Almost a full month after Kara had gotten out of the hospital, he and Rose had had lunch with her and Conner at the Golden Oar.

Kara had claimed she'd been desperate to get out into the real world again and was tired of being locked inside, unable to lift a finger. Her left arm was still wrapped in a green cast and held close to her body, as if she was concerned to move it.

"I wanted a burger," Kara said before sinking her teeth into the burger she'd ordered. Conner had helped her by cutting her burger into more manageable bites. "Mmm," she said, reaching for the chocolate shake.

"I drove Kara by the lot before heading over here for lunch," Conner said.

"I can't believe how much you guys have gotten done on it. And so quickly," Kara broke in.

"The weather has actually set us back some," Jacob admitted.

"Still, I can't wait to move in when it's done," Kara had added with a smile.

Rose glanced between Kara and Conner. "So, it's official." She smiled. "The two of you are really engaged?"

Kara smiled. "We're going ring shopping soon."

"After she's out of the cast," Conner broke in.

"And the swelling in my finger goes down." Kara looked down at her left hand.

Jacob noticed her wiggle the fingers slightly as she frowned down at her fingers.

"How's the dog?" Jacob asked.

Both his brother's and Kara's faces lit up.

"Great! We named him Shadow," Kara answered. "It fits him, since he follows Conner around everywhere."

"You got a dog?" Rose asked, sounding excited.

He smiled and tried to hide his excitement about Sophie, whom he had visited every day since choosing to adopt her. Each day he'd visited, he'd fallen more in love with the dog.

"Yes," Conner answered and filled Rose in on Shadow.

"I've been thinking of getting a dog myself. Maybe I'll head up to Carrie's and see if I can find one," Rose said, surprising him.

"What will your parents think about you having a dog at their place?" Conner asked her, and Jacob silently praised his brother's question since he'd wanted to know the answer as well.

Rose waved her hand and chuckled. "They have two dogs now themselves. I think there's still a few of Buster's things around the place somewhere."

"Buster was the little terrier you had?" Conner asked.

"Yeah." Rose's smile slipped slightly. "He died a few years back. That's when my parents got two corgis, Bert and Ernie." She held up her hand. "My dad named them. My mother and I had basically no input." She rolled her eyes with a chuckle.

"Did your parents get all moved into the rental?" Jacob asked Kara, changing gears.

Thankfully, the conversation switched away from the possibility of Rose adopting a dog to Kara's parents moving to Pride.

After lunch, they drove back up to the worksite in his truck. She'd gotten her truck back from the shop with a new rim on the wheel and insisted on driving to work each day separately. He figured it was to keep up appearances, but for lunch, he'd convinced her to ride along with him.

Work on the job site started at seven in the morning and continued sometimes until after seven at night. Workers tended to take their lunches on site and therefore the newly installed gate, which was put up to keep anyone out after hours and discourage people from roaming the construction site, was left open.

However, when they drove up after lunch, the gate was shut, and a large orange notice was taped over the lock.

"What the..." Jacob said, putting the truck into park and jumping out to read what the sign said.

"Someone's filed an injunction. Seriously?" Rose said from over his shoulder. "Now? After construction has already started?"

"I'm calling my uncle," he said, pulling out his phone.

An hour later, he stood in the courthouse building downtown with his uncle Todd, his aunt Lacey, and Rose.

Officially, they had gotten word that they had to wait a week for the injunction to be heard in front of the county judge in Edgeview, but since Lacey was the mayor of Pride and knew people, the case was moved up to two days from then.

They also had a copy of the legal paperwork, which Todd and his lawyer immediately started to scour.

"We'll deal with this," Todd assured him and Rose. "Until then..."

"Until then," the lawyer jumped in, "no one can set foot on the site or so much as pick up a hammer. You'll have to cancel all your contractors until this gets straightened out," the lawyer said.

"Right," Jacob said and pulled out his phone to let his guys know what was up.

Thirty phone calls later, he and Rose turned to go.

"My truck." She stopped and said to the lawyer, "My truck is still on the property. Can I..."

"Anything and everything on the property is locked up

tight. I'm sorry, until we go before the judge, we can't even so much as step foot on the land," the lawyer informed her.

"We'll get your truck back." Todd moved over and wrapped an arm around Rose. "Until then, you're welcome to borrow—"

"I'll drive her anywhere she wants to go," Jacob jumped in.

Todd nodded and ran his hands through his hair before lowering his voice. "Do you think this has anything to do with..."

He didn't even have to get the name Thomas Carson out before both Jacob and Rose were nodding.

"Yeah," Jacob interrupted. "We talked about it on the way over here. It's just up the scumball's alley to do something like this. A few of my guys told me there was a man in a suit driving around and telling them to pack up for the day. That's how he got everyone off site before the county police arrived to lock the place down." He sighed. "I had to assure a few of them that they'll be paid no matter if the work continues or not.

"Looks like we'll have a little break," he said to Rose as they drove back through town to her place.

"I am so pissed," she said, with a slight huff. "If I ever meet that man..."

He glanced over at her and smiled. She was biting her bottom lip, a move he knew she did when she was in deep concentration or concerned about something.

"Hey." He reached his hand over and touched her arm. "I'm sure this is just a slight bump in the road. There's no doubt my uncle will get things squared away in a few days, and we'll be back at work."

"What about all those people we've already sold homes to?" she said, and he could hear the weariness in her tone.

"They will just have to wait a few more days to know anything, like we will," he said as they pulled into the driveway. "This isn't the first time someone has tried to stop my family from doing something. The law will be on our side. My uncle made sure to abide by every law before moving forward with this project," he assured her as he shut off the truck. "What do you say we take a walk on the beach?" he asked suddenly.

He knew that she was too upset to settle down, and since they now had the rest of the day free, he wanted to enjoy the sunlight while they had it.

She glanced up at the house, and he could tell she was thinking the same thing. That if they went inside, they'd probably end up going stir crazy.

"Yeah," she said with a sigh, "that sounds like a good idea."

Until they reached the beach, they remained silent. He leaned over and took her hand in his as they started walking down the cold sand together.

"I don't know what I'd do if this fell through," she said, almost to herself.

He glanced down at her. "It won't."

She looked up at him. "How can you be so sure? I heard horror stories in school where construction sites were completely shut down due to lawsuits."

He shrugged. "My uncle is pretty confident in his lawyers. Besides, if this is Carson, something tells me the man hasn't got a clue as to what he's doing. He's probably throwing anything and everything he can come up with at us to try and get the land back. Maybe he thinks if he stops the subdivision from being built, that my uncle with sell him back the land for cheap." He shook his head.

She grew quiet for a while as they walked towards the

lighthouse and the construction land. They both looked up at the same time to the hillside.

A large gap in the trees was the only visible sign of the construction area so far. Soon, there would be homes on the hillside, but for now, the main roads had been laid, a few lots had been cleared, and three foundations had been poured.

They both stopped and continued to look up there. When he glanced over at Rose, tears were streaming down her cheeks.

"Hey," he said, pulling her into his arms, "what's this about?"

She shook her head and then buried her face into his shoulders. "It's all I have. I don't want to leave Pride so soon. I doubt I'll be able to find other work..."

"You're not leaving." He felt his heart skip at the thought of losing her so soon. Without realizing it, he'd made mental plans of being with her a lot longer. "Trust me, my uncle will find a way to make this go away. Even if it takes a while, he assured me that he's going to keep you here."

"He did?" she asked, frowning up at him.

He nodded. Okay, so it was a lie. But if he knew his uncle, which he did, then there was no way Todd Jordan was going to let Rose leave Pride. Not when he still wanted her to finish the job she'd started. Rose was like family to the Jordans. And there was one thing about his family that rang true. They took care of each other.

CHAPTER NINE

Rose knew that Jacob was trying to fill her free time to keep her mind off the fact that she may have very well lost everything she'd worked so hard for in the past few years.

Not to mention the possibility that she might have to move back to the city. Away from Pride, the people she cared for, the job she loved, and more importantly, away from Jacob.

Their first full day off the job together, he convinced her to repaint her bedroom and change her smaller bed for the bigger one that sat in the guest room down the hallway.

By the end of the day, his scheme had worked. Her bedroom was now painted a soft cream color and had a queen-sized bed. She'd also been too busy working all day, and then too tired when they were done, to think about anything else.

The following day, he convinced her to drive into the city to do a little shopping with Kara and Conner. The four of them spent a wonderful day in Portland, shopping and having lunch along the river. The only time she was alone with her thoughts was the long drive home, when the conversation was filled with Kara and her wedding plans.

It was as if everyone in the car knew not to talk about what was going on back in Pride. She had to admit, as she lay in bed with Jacob that night, that it felt wonderful to have people who cared so much about her that they would give up their day to help her keep her mind off of bad news.

The following day, Jacob's uncle would be in court, fighting for their futures. So when Jacob suggested they take a drive, she automatically turned him down.

They still had somehow ended up at Sara's Nook for breakfast and, after, at Carrie's Sanctuary.

"What are we doing here?" she said, feeling her heart sink at the knowledge that there was no way she would be able to adopt a dog now. Not when her own future was up in the air.

"Well, I wanted to introduce my two ladies to one another," Jacob said with a smile.

At first, his words hadn't registered. He was standing over a box of small puppies that were wobbling around as if they'd just learned how to walk. Her heart melted at the small puppies, but again, reality bit into her dreams. If she wasn't able to think about rescuing a dog, there was no way she would be able to get a puppy.

"This is Sophie," Jacob said, kneeling by the tan mother dog, who started licking Jacob's hand and wagging her tail.

"Hi, Sophie," Rose said softly. "Are you getting one of her puppies?" she asked Jacob.

"No." He shook his head. "Once all of her puppies have found their forever homes, I'm taking Sophie home with me." He leaned his head down and rubbed his face in the dog's golden fur.

Seeing Jacob's care and excitement for the older dog, Rose's heart melted.

Most men she'd known and dated would have overlooked the mother dog and gone for the big excitement of getting a puppy. But that wasn't Jacob. That wasn't the man she'd fallen in love with.

Their past may have been full of teasing and practical jokes, but behind it all, he'd been kind. He'd always gone out of his way to ensure there was kindness to animals and to those in need.

How many times had he apologized to her for scaring or upsetting her? Each and every time he'd done so, her heart had opened a little more to him, even though she had still believed him to be a royal pain in her butt. Now, however, she could look back on those times and truly laugh.

"You're adopting the mother?" she asked, kneeling beside the crate that held the family. Reaching out, she let the dog sniff her fingers. When Sophie butted her hand to allow her to pet her, she smiled.

"Yeah," Jacob said easily. "I sort of fell in love with her when I was here to pick up Conner and Kara's puppy a few weeks back. I've been coming here every day, and I'm going to keep visiting her until she's ready to take home."

Her chest tightened as she sat back and watched Jacob interact with Sophie. Just knowing that the two of them would have a future together, no matter what, reminded her that she might not have a future here herself.

They spent almost a full hour walking around and visiting all the animals at the sanctuary, then they drove into town to meet his uncle at the Golden Oar.

She hadn't expected to see her parents sitting at a large table with both Todd and Megan.

"Mom, Dad, what are you doing in town?" she asked, sliding into the chair next to her mother. Her mother gave her a hug before answering.

"Don't worry, we're just here for the day. Todd and Megan asked us to come down for lunch." Her mother motioned to the other couple.

"Well?" Jacob asked Todd after sitting at the table next to her. "What's the verdict?"

"We're all set. The case was thrown out when the other side didn't show up for court. After some deliberation and some investigation on my lawyer's part, we found out that the injunction was filed by Walter Stein."

Jacob took in the name and then started laughing. "You have got to be kidding me?"

Todd smiled as he shook his head.

"What's the joke?" Rose asked when it appeared she was the only one not in on the game.

"Walter B. Stein is an ass," Jacob said with a smile.

"Okay," she said slowly. "So, the man—"

"No," Todd broke in. "Literally, he's a donkey. Everyone who's been around Pride in the past three years knows that Kenny Stein left his property, which happens to border Hidden Cove's land, to his favorite donkey."

"Walter B. Stein?" she asked after a moment.

Todd's smile doubled. "Exactly. Carrie and Josh have Walter up at the sanctuary and have been taking care of him since Kenny passed away."

She tried to make sense of what they were saying. "So, a donkey filed an injunction to get us to stop building?"

"It would appear that someone found out who owned the property adjacent to ours and filed a bogus environmental and flooding injunction. The judge took one look at the case and broke out in laughter." Todd shook his head. "Of course, now it's up to us to prove who really filed the paperwork."

"We're all set to get back to work then?" Jacob asked.

"Aiden's up there removing the locks as we speak," Todd assured them.

It was like a weight had been lifted from her chest. She wanted to jump up from the table and do a booty dance, but since her parents and the Jordans were there, she settled for a fist pump and a high five with Jacob. Which of course drew the eye of both her parents and his uncle and aunt.

"The two of you seem to be getting along much better," her father pointed out as he glanced between the pair of them.

"We've learned to not kill one another," she admitted. She avoided her father's eyes and pulled up the menu to block his gaze.

The entire lunch, she itched to get up to the site and back to work. And back to her own truck too. Of course, the lunch conversation was filled with speculation on who had really filed the lawsuit.

"We all know Thomas Carson wouldn't hesitate to stoop to this level. After all, if he's the one who hired and killed Kurt Collins, the man who we assume shot Kara, then a lawsuit is right up his alley," Todd said.

Everyone in town had heard how the blue truck's owner had driven off the highway shortly after Kara's shooting. The truck had ended up on the rocky shoreline off Highway One just inside the California boarder. Which left more questions about the shooting.

"The real question is, what will his next move be?" Jacob pointed out.

"Well, the judge has agreed to flag any other lawsuits against us filed by a donkey," Todd said with a smile. "But something tells me that it won't stop Carson from using another name or, god forbid, actually convincing a property owner to file against us."

"What about Kara and Robin's land? Has Robin had any issues since her sister was shot?" Rose's mother asked.

"No, but since I've had private security watching their property, I doubt he'll make a move on them again. Especially since everyone in town is on the lookout for the man," Todd answered.

"Still, I could..." Rose's mother started to say.

"No," her dad jumped in. "Honey, I think they have it under control. We're supposed to be in Paris this weekend, remember?"

Her mother's smile grew. "Paris," she added with a sigh.

"Besides," Ric said, taking his wife's hand, "I think Todd has learned enough from you over the years to have this situation under control."

"I have my best men watching Robin and Kara." He grinned. "My nephews."

"Your most annoying men is more like it," Jacob added. "I hear George is pissing Robin off by constantly being underfoot."

"I hear," Rose jumped in, defending George, who happened to be one of her all-time favorite Jordan men, "that George is helping out while Kara is healing. Kara couldn't talk kindly enough about how he's stepped up to help around the venue, all while keeping an eye on her sister. I know she feels safer knowing Robin is being watched out for." She said the last to Todd. "And I know they are both grateful for the extra protection. Which you didn't have to do."

Todd smiled at her. "It's really great to have you around. I think you level Jacob out." Todd's eyes narrowed at Jacob.

She tried to hide her smile. Jacob nudged her under the table, which made her smile even more.

As Jacob drove back to the job site, Rose tried to contain her excitement at returning to work.

"You know," he said, glancing over at her, "you shouldn't encourage my family."

She glanced over at him. "Encourage?"

"You know, as far as..." He motioned quickly between them.

Her eyebrows shot up and her temper started to flare.

"Oh. I wasn't aware that is what I was doing," she said in a clipped voice that he didn't seem to notice.

"They have already been all over me since Thanksgiving. I mean, I tell them I'm staying with a friend, then your parents come into town, forcing me to return home..." He glanced over at her again. "They have their suspicions."

What was he saying? Was he actually hiding their relationship from them? Why?

Sure, it was true that they hadn't officially made their relationship public, but it wasn't as if she was trying to hide it either. Was he?

"I wasn't aware we were trying to keep them from knowing," she said softly.

Instead of answering right away, he parked his truck beside hers and turned the engine off. Then he turned to her and ran his eyes slowly over her.

"I thought it's what you wanted."

Was it? She'd been enjoying their time together. The dynamics of their relationship. How it had been just the two of them. She knew his family. Knew that if they made their relationship public, things could get complicated.

The conversation dampened her excitement to return to work. For the rest of the day, those thoughts of taking the next step by telling his family loomed over her like a large cloud over her head.

CHAPTER TEN

He didn't know what he'd said or done, but he knew full well that Rose was upset at him. He'd known her long enough to understand when she was pissed at him. It was just like before they'd started seeing one another. He still had no clue why she was acting the way she was.

One moment everything was perfect, and the next, she was locked in her office, sulking.

Since they only had half a day back on the jobsite, he was flooded with incoming calls, and also had to return calls and respond to emails from his contractors.

It was hell trying to coordinate and get all his crew back on the jobsite first thing in the morning. Most of the contractors had scheduled other jobs in the short time they'd been down, as it hadn't been clear when they would be able to be back at work.

But after a few hours of working and persuading everyone they were back one hundred percent, he was finally prepared for work to pick up again first thing in the morning.

Just before five, he knocked on Rose's office door and

opened it to see her sitting at her computer, engrossed in what was on the screen.

She glanced up at him and waited for him to talk.

"I was going to head out and visit Sophie again. She likes to go on afternoon walks to stretch her legs," he said, hoping she would offer to go with him. Instead, she nodded and glanced back down at her screen. "You, uh... will you need a ride?"

"I have my truck," she said without looking up.

He wanted to ask her if everything was okay but was afraid of her answer. Yet his feet were rooted to the spot. He didn't want to leave, knowing she was upset at him.

He tried to go over their last conversation in his head, looking for any signs of what he'd said or done to upset her.

His heart sank when he realized he couldn't find anything and that maybe it was just him. Maybe she'd grown bored of him? Bored of their time together?

It was as if his body moved on its own. One minute he was leaning on the door jamb, the next he was beside her, pulling her chair out and pulling her up into his arms.

He crushed her mouth under his, holding her, wishing to show her just how much she meant to him. His mind registered that her body had gone lax at first, but as he pinned her between his body and the desk, her arms slowly traveled up until she circled them around his shoulders.

When a sexy soft moan escaped from her, he gripped her hips and hoisted her to sit on the edge of the desk. Her legs wrapped around him and he felt his body instantly react to her softness against him.

"Rose." Her name came out as a whisper against her skin as she tugged first his jacket, then his shirt off his shoulders.

"Here, now," she said eagerly. "Jacob, I need..." She

stopped to run her teeth over his exposed collarbone. "You," she finished as she looked into his eyes.

Instantly, he wished he'd locked the door to the trailer, but then he smiled when he remembered that currently, there weren't any workers on site. There wouldn't be until the following morning. The chances of them being caught were very slim. Slim enough that he was willing to chance it. Besides, he would hear the gravel outside crunch loudly under the tires if anyone drove up.

When her nails scraped across his ribs, he growled and stood her up. Then in one quick move, he yanked her jeans off her narrow hips and spun her around until she leaned on the edge of her desk. Her jeans pooled around her work boots, trapping her legs as she arched backwards closer to him. Her long dark hair fanned out on the desk.

But he was too far gone for finesse. He wanted her just as much as she wanted him. In record time, he had her bare skin against his as he sheathed himself fully into her.

She arched back into him, crying out his name as she gripped the desk and moaned with his movements. She was begging him to move faster, harder. Egging him to completely lose control. If he thought about it, he had done that the first time he'd kissed her.

Reaching up, he leaned into her, cupped her perfect breasts in his hands and felt himself release as she tightened around him and cried out his name.

"So," he said moments later, his forehead resting against the back of her shoulder while he bent over her. She was lying facedown over her desk, and he was still fully embedded in her. "Are we good?"

He waited, counting his heartbeats before she answered.

"Yeah, we're good," she said finally with a sigh. "I'll see

you at home later," she said softly. "I have some work to catch up on here."

He nodded and then quickly pulled away. He didn't even wait to see her dress quickly. Instead, he pulled up his pants and left.

He wasted as much time as he could up at Carrie's Sanctuary before driving over to his parents' place. He was hoping to get a little inside information as to what Rose expected from him by talking to his mother. But watching how perfect his parents' relationship was just left him even more frustrated.

He still didn't know if Rose wanted him to tell his family about their relationship or not. Which meant, his conversation with his mother was very cryptic.

By the time he left his parents' place, he figured that either his mother knew about him and Rose and was just leading him to believe she didn't, or she was too worried about getting everything ready for Christmas to really focus on their conversation.

When he arrived at Rose's place, she was already in bed and fast asleep.

The following morning came too early, and the next day was so busy trying to catch up from the time off that there hadn't been a moment to even talk about work, let alone a chance to ask her how she felt personally.

She had several errands that had her away most of the day anyway. Both he and Rose had been working from sunup to long after sundown most days, including week-ends, just to play catch-up on the half dozen homes that had been started. Not to mention the clubhouse and other facili-ties that were being built in the neighborhood.

One day turned into two, which turned into a week and, suddenly, Christmas was upon them and he hadn't even had time to even think about shopping for her or anyone else in his family.

Sophie wouldn't be ready to come home for a few more weeks, which meant he would have to come up with another option for making Rose's Christmas special.

He knew that Rose had fallen head over heels for the mother dog. The only personal time they'd had together was when they visited Sophie almost daily. That time was filled with visiting the dog or chatting with Carrie and Josh. They had yet to fully discuss sharing their relationship with others. He continued to steer clear of the subject, which seemed to keep them both happy, if not distant.

Something told him everyone in town already knew they were an item, but they hadn't made it official yet. In his mind, that was her move, not his.

He'd known Rose his entire life and had never had an issue talking with her before now. But each time he thought to bring up the subject, he became tongue-tied, or he grew confused at what words to say.

He was acting like a schoolboy trying to talk to his first crush. It irritated him so much that he pushed the entire scenario to the back of his mind.

After all, he was happy—really happy—with Rose. Why on earth would he want to mess anything up?

He spent his first official day off in weeks scouring through what felt like every store in Edgeview in hopes that he would find the perfect gift for Rose. He found a ton of perfect smaller gifts for her, trinkets that reminded him of long past summer days or fun events they'd shared in the past.

By the time he was done shopping, the entire cab of his truck was filled with gifts. A lot of the bags were filled with items for Rose but most were for his large family, which helped drain his bank account.

Thankfully, he remembered that his cousin Lilly and his sister Riley were offering free gift wrapping at their boutique, Classy and Sassy. He'd purchased a lot of the gifts from their store, and he dropped off the rest of the gifts with them to be wrapped and delivered to the house just in time for the family gathering. All except one special gift he'd gotten for Rose. That one he wanted to wrap himself.

He figured it was time to come clean to his family. After all, they would be spending the entire holiday weekend with both of their families and there was no way he was going to try and hide what she'd come to mean to him.

He doubted he was a good enough actor to hide it from all of his family members anyway.

He knew Rose's parents were due to arrive in Pride later that evening and had arranged to spend the next few nights back in his old childhood bedroom.

When he walked into the house, the smell of home cooking hit him, and he realized that he hadn't even stopped to grab some lunch while shopping.

He supposed he'd been too worried about picking out the perfect gift to focus on anything else all day long.

He wondered if Rose had been trying to find him a gift. They'd briefly talked about being together with both of their families this year since his mother had invited her family over for the massive Jordan Clan Holiday Hang, as everyone had been calling it for years.

This Christmas, his parents were hosting the gathering themselves at their home. Which meant, from the moment he walked into his house, he had to make sure not to leave so much as a fingerprint on any clean surface.

He even went as far as to remove his shoes before stepping inside. His father was busy at the stove, and his mother was putting the finishing touches on a pie that she'd pulled from the oven.

"Something smells wonderful," he said, getting his mother's attention. Walking over, he stepped within eyesight of his father and received a smile and a nod from him.

"Smells good," Jacob signed to his father.

"Your father can't stop stirring," his mother said from behind him, "or the cream will curdle." "Today is baking day."

"I can see that." He walked over and, even though he knew better, he dipped his finger into the scraped-clean bowl of homemade whipped cream.

Instead of scolding him, his mother handed him the bowl. "It's a good thing you're here now. You can clean up." He took the bowl from her and scraped the remaining cream from the bottom before washing it along with several other bowls and utensils that filled the sink.

The standing rule in the Jordan house was that if you weren't the one who cooked, you cleaned. Needless to say, the majority of the time when he'd been growing up, he'd done dishes along with his brother and sister.

"So, how long are you back to stay this time?" his father signed to him when they were all sitting around the table for dinner.

He thought about it, knowing full well that Rose's parents were planning on staying through the New Year.

Instead of answering, he shrugged and avoided his parents' eyes.

"We aren't as blind as you think we are," his mother said softly. When he glanced up at her, she was smiling back at him.

"Yeah, I figured," he said with another shrug.

"Why the secrecy?" his father asked.

"It's what Rose wants," he answered quickly.

When both of his parents' eyebrows shot up, he questioned if they knew something that he didn't.

"Why? What did you hear?" he asked, setting down his fork. His father had made yet another wonderful meal, and Jacob was already on his second helping.

His mother glanced over at his dad and then shrugged.

"Hear? Nothing really, it's just..."

"Mom?" He waited.

She sighed and set her own fork down. "You know that the Derbys are longtime friends of ours."

"Yes." He was starting to grow impatient.

"It's just that they mentioned that they thought that Rose was seeing someone, and we put two and two together. At first your father was worried." She glanced over at his dad, who nodded slightly as he read her lips. "I finally convinced him that this could be a good thing. I mean, the two of you have been skirting around one another forever."

"Skirting..." He shook his head with a chuckle. "We've been at each other's throats all our lives."

"Which is why we were worried at first," his mother added. "But in the past couple months..." Had it really been that long, he wondered while his mother continued on. "Well, we've..." She shook her head quickly. "Everyone has seen the improvements. The changes in how you treat each other."

"It's the reason Ric and Rob decided to come down here for the holidays instead of getting Rose to return to Portland," his father signed.

He held in a groan. Great. He should have been more careful what he wished for. He'd wanted everyone to know about them and now that they did... well, now he was wishing for their privacy. Especially, after his mother started asking questions about their relationship.

Instead of answering, he picked up his plate and started clearing up the dishes.

He could tell that his parents were having a silent conversation behind him. Signing to one another. He figured his father was trying to convince his mother to butt out.

When he was done cleaning his dish, he turned back to them. "The truth is, I'm not sure Rose wants everything about us out in the open."

"Have you asked her?" his mother asked.

"N-no," he said truthfully. "But something tells me that she was hoping it would remain just between us. I mean, the Jordans are a little..." He motioned to the massive kitchen with all of its perfect decorations. "Overwhelming," he finally finished. He leaned against the counter and crossed his arms over his chest, suddenly feeling very tired.

His mother stood up and walked over to wrap her arms around him. He rested his chin on the top of her head and closed his eyes at the comforting feeling of holding his mother.

Her soft scent floated up and surrounded him as much as her arms did his waist.

"She's been around us all her life. I would think that by now, she's used to our...quirks." She pulled back and smiled up at him.

He smiled at that, then thought about Rose. About the possibility of his family screwing this up for him.

"It means something," he said softly.

His mother laughed again. "Course it does. You're a Jordan."

"What does that mean?" he asked, pulling back further.

"Jordan men are well..." She looked over to his dad for help. She signed to him, and Iian Jordan stood up and walked over to them.

"Screwed," he finished for her as he slapped Jacob on the shoulder.

"Iian." His mother nudged his dad in the chest playfully.

"When it comes to relationships, there's only one woman per Jordan man," his father signed quickly. He wrapped his arms around his mother's waist, then said out loud, "When you find her, all you can do is hold on and enjoy the ride."

CHAPTER ELEVEN

Rose really enjoyed having a few days off. Work had been crazy for the past few weeks after they'd been shut down. She'd spent hours at the city and county buildings trying to push permits through, getting foundation inspections, or just waiting on planning approval for the half dozen homes she'd sold recently.

She spent her first day off shopping in Edgeview. She'd had no clue what to get her parents for the holidays, but luckily she'd convinced Suzie, whom Rose had been close friends with all of her life, to tag along with her for the shopping trip.

Suzie had come up with the idea of turning an old family photo of the family on the Oregon beach at sunset into one of those large canvases that her parents could hang over their fireplace.

The large wrapped framed picture sat in the back seat of her truck, along with several other gifts for the Jordan family.

"Are you sure you didn't need anything?" she asked her friend.

"No." Suzie chuckled. "I finished my holiday shopping months ago." She smiled. "I just picked up my last Christmas gift yesterday."

"Seriously? You have had all your shopping done for months?" she asked, feeling a little overwhelmed at the idea that she'd forgotten someone on her list.

There were a lot of Jordans to buy for, so she'd settled for getting something unique for each family and something small for every child. It was more fun to watch kids open wrapped gifts than adults. Of course, Jacob had been particularly hard to buy for. It had taken sneaking away from Suzie in the massive store at the mall to look for something just for him. She'd had a few moments of panic when she'd questioned her gift idea, but then she took several deep breaths and decided to go with her first instincts.

Which, of course, had her wondering what Jacob was getting her for Christmas. She tried not to focus too much on that, since it made her nervous to know that her family and all of his would know that they were officially an item.

What would they think? Would they warn them from seeing one another? Did his family already know? Part of her suspected it. Part of her feared it.

Not that she didn't love the Jordan clan. But facts were facts. She'd been raised around all of them. She knew all their quirks, all their personalities, more than most families knew one another.

She loved each and every one of them just as much as she loved her own mother and father.

Glancing over quickly at Suzie, she realized that there had been a time when Rose had dreamed that they were sisters, along with all the other Jordan girls. Rose had wanted a sister so badly that she hadn't minded that she had only been able to see them during the summer months.

"What do you say we stop off and grab burgers before heading back to Pride?" Suzie asked. Rose instantly felt her stomach growl loudly.

"Sounds like a plan." She pulled into the parking lot of one of her favorite burger places.

Over food, they chatted about Suzie's wedding and honeymoon. Then, somehow, the conversation turned towards work and Suzie tactfully—well, as tactfully as possible—brought up her and Jacob.

"So, you and Jacob, huh?" Suzie said just after Rose had taken a large sip of soda. The next moment, root beer was shooting out of Rose's nose as she coughed and sputtered. The sting caused her eyes to tear up and water.

"Easy," Suzie said, reaching over and slapping her on her back several times. "I didn't mean to scare you."

Rose took a deep breath and settled down after taking another sip of her soda, making sure to swallow correctly this time.

"I mean," Suzie started again, "the entire family kind of already knows."

"They do?" she asked a little shocked. No one had led on that they knew that there was anything between her and Jacob, at least not to her.

"Sure. I mean, no one is quite sure when it started, but my aunt and uncle seem to think he's actually been living with you." Suzie stilled and watched Rose's face carefully. When Rose didn't say anything, she narrowed her eyes at her. "He has?" she asked after a moment. Then her smile was quick. "He has," she accused as she leaned forward on the table. "Since when?"

Rose shrugged. "Since before Thanksgiving sometime," she admitted.

Suzie smiled. "How wonderful."

"No." She shook her head. "Don't make this something it isn't," she warned.

"Oh?" Suzie leaned back. "Like what?"

"We're just..." She started feeling a little frustrated. "Together."

The truth was, she knew that she wanted more with Jacob. After all, she'd been in love with him her entire life.

But to hope that he felt the same way about her, well, that was just dreaming. After all, only a few short months ago they'd been at one another's throats, fighting over anything and everything.

As she drove back to Pride, she kept wondering just when things had changed in Jacob's mind about her. The fear was there as well, and she wondered if he could easily change his mind back about her.

Sure, there were times he still annoyed the hell out of her. He was so nonchalant about certain things, things she knew they couldn't afford to waver on. Then he would get worked up when she would require him to slow down and take the time to hash out all the details.

It was one of the only things they argued about any more. That and when he wanted to talk about their relationship, and she avoided him. What was she supposed to say? She didn't know if they should tell his family.

Fear was her driving factor now. She didn't want anything to come between her and the rest of the Jordans. What if something went wrong between her and Jacob?

She couldn't afford to lose her position with his family. Not when they held all the keys to her future.

Part of her doubted that Jacob's uncle would be so vicious as to fire her if they ever broke up, but another part of her knew that his family was very tight. The most important thing to her was not to make it weird between their two families.

After dropping Suzie off, she drove back home. She held in a soft groan when she noticed her parents' car in the driveway.

Leaving their present in the truck, she gathered the rest of the smaller gifts, hoping to have time to wrap them later that night.

"Mom? Dad?" she called out when she stepped inside. Instantly, she was attacked by Bert and Earnie. Setting down the bags, she laughed as the two dogs licked her.

"In here," her mother called from in the kitchen.

She picked up both dogs and stepped into the kitchen. She set the dogs down when they wiggled in her arms.

"Where's Dad?" she asked, walking over to hug her mother.

"He's upstairs showering. We just got here about an hour ago, and he needed to clean up while I make us some dinner."

"Smells good," she said as she sat down at the kitchen bar.

"So, I noticed you moved some furniture around?" Her mother glanced over her shoulder at her.

"Yeah." She had already thought up what she'd tell her parents about redecorating. "The old mattress wasn't cutting it any longer. Besides, I was tired of the pink walls and since I had a few days off when things were shut down"—she shrugged—"I figured I'd get it all done at once."

"It looks good," her mother said. "I hope you don't mind, but I took a peek."

"No," she said quickly. Before she'd left that morning, she'd made sure all of Jacob's things were tucked away, out of eyesight. Not that she believed her parents to be snoopy people, but she figured she'd play it safe. "If you were looking for your present..." she teased, "I hadn't bought it yet."

Her mother smiled. "No, that wasn't it."

"Snooping?" she asked.

Her mother chuckled. "No, I was just curious as to why my guest room was missing a bed."

"I planned on replacing it when I had time," she admitted.

"Don't worry about it," her mother said. "Your dad has been wanting to turn that room in to an office for years." She rolled her eyes. "Now he has an excuse to do so."

Just then her dad jogged down the stairs and engulfed her in a hug. "I thought I heard the dogs barking," he said after kissing the top of her head. "Something smells good." He turned to her mom and then kissed her.

"I know it's a couple days early, but I figured we could have our own little Christmas dinner. Just the three of us." Her mother amended her statement when Bert and Earnie barked. "The five of us."

Rose couldn't help but smile. For months she'd been missing the companionship of the little fur balls.

While enjoying dinner with her family, she kept thinking about Jacob and his love for Sophie. What would her parents think of him and another dog living there, in their home?

It wasn't as if Jacob and she had discussed hiding the fact that he was living there from her parents.

She'd informed him that her parents would be arriving later that day, and he'd packed up his bag of clothes and had left shortly before she'd gotten out of the shower.

He'd done the same for Thanksgiving, and she knew that once her parents left after the New Year, he'd be back without any discussion between them. It wasn't an awkward thing, but more like an unspoken agreement.

Any time they started talking about their relationship and where it was going, she feared that the possibilities of her heart being broken were high. So she avoided it, and anytime he hinted at the topic, she changed it or avoided him by burying herself in her work.

She liked the way things were between them. Sure, she wanted to know where things stood when it came to their future together. But she wasn't willing to chance him breaking things off with her just yet.

She would have thought that her desire for him would have dissipated over time, but the fact was, if anything, it had just grown more ferocious the longer she was with him.

"You're deep in thought," her dad said as she helped him clean up after dinner. Her mother was sitting in front of the fire her dad had built earlier, watching the news.

Biting her lower lip, she decided she could at least hint at what she wanted. She knew that there was no way she would be able to keep the news that she was seeing Jacob after the large family gathering in a few days.

"I'm thinking of getting a dog," she blurted out.

Her father's eyebrows shot up. "Okay," he said slowly. "You know this place is as much yours as it is ours. You don't have to ask our permission..."

"No, it's not that," she said, shaking her head.

Her dad studied her face. "Then?" he asked after a moment of silence.

"I mean, I know I have the run of the place." She took a deep breath. "It's just..."

"She's trying to tell us that Jacob's been staying over here," her mother said from the other room.

"I know that." Her father rolled his eyes as he smiled at

her. "I'm just letting her take her time doing so," he called back to her mother.

Rose crossed her arms over her chest. "How did... You already knew?" She felt her face heat.

"Honey, you do remember that I was a detective before I met your father?" Her mother muted the television and came back into the kitchen to wrap her arms around her. "We didn't mean to spoil your surprise..."

"It wasn't a surprise," she broke in quickly. This time it was her mother's eyebrows that shot up.

"Oh?" she asked.

"More like a..." she started.

"Secret?" her dad supplied.

"No." She shook her head, unable to come up with the words to explain why she'd hidden her relationship with Jacob. Other than fear.

"I know that the Jordans can be a little... overwhelming when it comes to certain things. But, if you and Jacob want privacy, I'm sure they will abide by your wishes," her mother said.

"It's not that either. At least, I don't think so." Her parents were quiet for a moment. "I think I messed this up," she exclaimed as she threw her hands up in frustration. She paced as she explained to her parents all her fears about her and Jacob's relationship.

CHAPTER TWELVE

To say that the house was a little chaotic Christmas day would have been a total understatement. Every single room downstairs was filled with family members. The young kids were corralled into the family room where they were entertained with opening gifts, playing games, and watching cartoons.

The adults, having decided to allow the younger kids to enjoy their gifts first, were busy eating and chatting with one another. The noise level had Jacob's ears ringing, so he took a moment to let his parents' dogs out back and enjoy the quiet of the snow falling. The two young Lab mix brothers were a handful, but totally lovable. They were far too hyper to be around this many people and had been locked in the laundry room during the party.

Someone else stepped outside shortly after him, and he glanced over to see Ric Derby pulling on his coat and heading his way.

Jacob had been warned, via a text message yesterday, that Rose's parents knew all about their relationship. It appeared that everyone in Pride knew about them. Here they were, believing they had been keeping it to themselves. He was slightly shocked that everyone around them let them continue to believe it.

"Guess we got that white Christmas everyone was hoping for." Ric stopped beside him as Snoops, one of his parents' dogs, came up and sniffed his leg. Ric bent down and scratched the mutt's fur. "Is this Sneak or Snoop?" he asked him.

"Snoops," he answered. "Sneak has a little white star on his chest." He motioned to the other dog, which was currently peeing on the pile of wood.

"Right." Ric straightened. "Any hint as to what their names mean?"

He shrugged and chuckled. "My parents' idea of their personalities." He shook his head then glanced over at the man. "How are Bert and Earnie?"

Ric laughed. "Touché." He slapped Jacob on the shoulder. "Rose has informed us that you're getting one of the new homes up at Hidden Cove?"

"Yeah." He felt his heart skip. He'd prepared for this conversation with the man. The one where Ric asked him his intentions for his daughter. Hell, he didn't know himself. The only thing that he was certain of was that he wanted to be with Rose.

Ric turned slightly to him. "Which model did you pick out?"

"The Starfish." He held in a chuckle at the name Rose had chosen for the floorplan.

Ric nodded. "Nice. That was one of my favorites. Course, I always thought it should have a fireplace just inside the back door."

"Rose added one for me. One of those types that, if we lose power, it doubles as a stove." He bent down and tossed a stick for Sneak. The dog was a stick-aholic and would play toss for hours or until the person throwing it gave up. "Put a fancy stone fireplace in the main bedroom too."

He had been so busy entertaining the dog that he hadn't seen Ric's reaction as he'd spoken. But now he glanced over at the man, who appeared thoughtful. Jacob instantly wondered what he'd said.

Then it hit him. He'd said, *if we lose power*. Not *if I lose power*. Shit. Heat flooded his face and suddenly he wished to tug off the thick coat he'd pulled on to ward off the cold. Figuring the next words anyone said would decide how the rest of his life would go, he held his breath and waited.

"Rose said you're thinking of getting a dog yourself?" Ric nodded to the two dogs playing tug a war over the stick Jacob had just thrown.

Jacob relaxed. "Sophie's a five-year-old Lab mix. She's just had a litter of pups, so she won't be ready to come home for another few weeks." He melted a little as he talked about the dog.

"Well, just so you know, we've already okayed it with Rose." Ric turned to him and held out a hand to him.

Jacob took it without hesitation and shook it. Memories of doing the very same thing his entire life at various ages of his childhood surfaced quickly. How many times had Ric Derby done just that? Too many to count. Yet, somehow, this time it felt different. It felt... like a promise.

"I guess I'd better get back inside. I hear someone was about to cut into the pie," he said with a wink. Before he turned, he bent down and tossed the stick to the waiting dogs. "I miss having dogs that will chase sticks. Bert and Earnie are far too lazy." He chuckled as he walked back to the house.

"That wasn't too bad," Rose said after her father disappeared into the house.

Jacob turned and watched as she stepped out from behind a thick tree trunk.

"Were you hiding back there?" he asked, wondering why the dogs hadn't noticed her there and then wondering how long she'd been standing there without him noticing.

"Not hiding so much as... avoiding interrupting," she said with a shrug as she moved closer to him.

She'd pulled on a bright red jacket with a black fuzzy collar and a matching red beanie with her long dark hair tucked under it.

The falling snow had piled up on the top of her hat, and he surmised she'd been out there long enough to hear the entire exchange with her father.

She surprised him by walking directly up to him and wrapping her arms around his waist.

"So, my dad didn't kill you." She smiled up at him.

He chuckled. "No. And I'm very thankful for it. After all, my pride would have let him."

"Oh?" she asked, her eyebrows arching up.

"Yeah." He sighed and held onto her. "I should have asked—"

"Jacob Jordan. If you say the word permission, I'm going to..." He watched anger flood her eyes and couldn't stop himself from bending down and covering her mouth with his.

It had been two days and two long nights since he'd held her and just feeling her body next to his now warmed him thoroughly.

"Let's take a walk," he said softly when she pulled back. "The dogs are restless."

"Okay." She nodded as he took her gloved hand.

They walked in silence as the dogs darted around them on the short trail that went between all the Jordan homes. At one point, he'd helped pour gravel on the dirt pathways since the family used them so often. Now the path was covered in fresh snow, but since he could probably walk them in his sleep, he headed towards the pond closest to his Aunt Lacy and Uncle Aaron's place.

"This is one of my favorite places," Rose said when they stopped by the water's edge.

Both dogs decided the water was too cold to jump in, and he was thankful since he didn't want to add giving them a bath to his chores when he returned home. Instead, they darted around and chased the mourning doves that had roosted for the winter in the nearby bushes.

He pulled Rose into his arms. "So, it appears that our secret is out." He searched her eyes.

"Yes," she said with a slight nod. "Are you okay with it?"

He could hear the uncertainty in her tone.

"Yes. You?" he asked.

She shrugged. "I don't really think it was ever a secret." She smiled up at him. "I mean, from what everyone is saying, they've suspected we were an item for a while."

"Is that what we are?" he asked, his heart skipping a beat in his chest while he waited for her response.

"I suppose so. I don't think going steady is a term used any longer," she said jokingly.

He smiled. "I swear, my heart skipped a few beats when your dad followed me outside."

She smiled up at him. "Afraid of a man double your age?"

"Hell no," he said with a laugh. "It's your mom that's the scary one."

She laughed even more. "Okay, there is some truth to

that," she admitted, and then she rested her head on his shoulder. "Is it wrong of me to say that I can't wait for them to go back to Portland?"

He sighed and held onto her. "I'll agree to that."

They stood there, in the silence of the woods, listening to the dogs chasing birds, watching the snow fall on the small pond, and silently wishing the moment could last forever.

Then her cell phone rang, breaking the silence, and she sighed.

"It's my mom," she said before answering it.

He half listened to her talk and when she hung up, they headed back to the house to join in the fun of opening more presents.

He stopped her from stepping in the back door.

"I have a couple gifts for you." He thought about her opening all of the small items he'd picked out for her in front of his family and hers and cringed. "I'd like to give you one of them in private. Do you think you can stick around after everyone leaves?"

She nodded. "I was going to give you yours when we were alone as well." She practically purred the words, which had his body responding.

"Oh?" he asked, pulling her closer. "Maybe we should wait..."

Just then, the back door flung open and his sister stood there, looking at them.

"Will the two of you hurry up? Everyone is waiting," Riley said as she rolled her eyes at him. "And I can't wait any longer to open my gifts." She slammed the door on them again.

He chuckled. "Riley could never wait to open presents."

For the next two hours, they sat around the large living room as everyone unwrapped gifts and ate pie.

At one point, Rose climbed into his lap, since there was a serious lack of seats around the large Christmas tree. He held onto her and enjoyed the feeling of being this close to her and not caring who knew they were together.

After his family started leaving, Rose helped his mother put the dishes away. The majority of the dishes had been cleaned after the main meal. He helped his father return the furniture to its rightful place, since they'd moved the chairs into the living room to seat everyone.

"So," his father signed to him after they'd returned all of the chairs to the formal dining room, "Ric had a chat with you?"

Jacob nodded and then signed back, "Yeah, he heard about my place up in Hidden Cove and me getting Sophie."

His father's smile grew. "Did you think he was going to punch you?"

"The thought had crossed my mind." He shrugged. "Maybe once or twice."

His father laughed and slapped him on the shoulder. "Ric has known you since the day you were born. You are as much his as you are ours." Jacob's heart did a little flip. "Just like Rose is part of us."

Jacob couldn't help it. He felt his entire being warm. Just knowing how little of a deal his family had made it somehow made things... smoother between him and Rose.

"I know," he signed back to his dad.

"Relax, whatever happens between you two, you'll always be family," his father added before turning and walking away.

"How about another walk?" he asked Rose as he stepped in the kitchen. "I can hear the dogs begging to go out from here." He chuckled as he started walking towards the laundry room where both dogs were whining to be let out.

"I hated putting them up, but they're so hyper around the little kids," his mother said, glancing over at him. "We took them on a long walk this morning in hopes that we'd wear them out. I can't wait until they get out of the terrible-two stage. They're still just puppies, no matter how big they are now."

He opened the laundry room door and both dogs bolted towards the back door. He grabbed Rose's coat, which she'd hung on the hook by the door, and helped her pull it on before grabbing up his own coat, hat, and gloves.

"It hasn't let up out there," Rose said, shoving her hair under her hat.

"No," he said with a smile.

"I have snow boots." His mother nodded to the pair by the back door. "You're welcome to wear them."

"Thanks." Rose shoved his mother's boots on her feet as he pulled on his father's pair that always sat by the back door in the winter.

Taking her gloved hand, they stepped out into the cold evening as he flipped on the floodlights that cast the entire backyard in bright light.

"Wow," Rose sighed. "It's like a winter wonderland out here."

The dogs, having finished their immediate business, were now dancing around the backyard in search of sticks and balls and smelling everything not covered with snow.

"It's one of my favorite times of year," he admitted. "How about we head down towards the beach?"

As with before, they walked in silence, with the dogs trailing behind them or rushing around them on the pathway that led down to the snow-covered sand and the water's edge.

He'd been nervous about giving her most of the gifts he'd picked out for her, but there was one gift in particular he was anxious about. Since the rest of the gifts were fun and lighthearted, he'd allowed her to open them while surrounded by family.

He'd gotten her a tool set in hot pink, which he figured she could leave in her truck since she was always borrowing his tools.

Most of the gifts she'd gotten him had been for Sophie. A new memory foam dog bed, food and water bowls with her name on them, and a bedazzled hot pink collar, which he'd laughed at so much, his family had looked at him strangely.

He wanted it to be a special moment, however, when he gave this last gift to her.

Stopping on the hillside that overlooked the water, he turned to her.

"I left out one gift," he said, pulling out the small wrapped box he'd placed in his jacket pocket earlier.

"So did I," she said with a smile, pulling out her own small wrapped gift.

They exchanged gifts and he waited until she started opening the box. Then she looked over at him.

"Let's do this together," she said, nodding towards his gift.

He unwrapped his gift and smiled down at the simple silver key on a keyring with etched letters reading Jacob, Rose, and Sophie.

He smiled over to Rose to thank her and saw her frowning down at her gift.

CHAPTER THIRTEEN

Rose's heart did an odd little flip. She couldn't believe what she was seeing. It was a simple black jewelry box. What exactly had Jacob given her? He couldn't be proposing to her now, could he? Here? Now? Like this? So soon?

"What..." she started to ask as she glanced up at him.

He stuffed the key and key ring she'd gotten him into his pocket and then tucked the wrapping paper and box into his jacket before reaching over and flipping the lid to the small jewelry box.

She took a deep breath of relief when she saw the silver chain tucked inside. Reaching in, she took out the necklace as the light shone on the pink heart diamond dangling from it.

Smiling, she allowed him to secure it around her neck.

When he placed a soft kiss on her exposed skin, she closed her eyes and held in a soft groan.

"My heart," he said softly, "as a promise that, no matter what happens, you will always hold it."

She melted. Quite literally, her entire being shifted

towards him as if she'd released the last hold on her own heart.

"Jacob." She turned towards him as he leaned in and brushed his lips over hers.

"God, I wish I could hold you tonight," he said with a sigh.

"Me too." She relaxed into his arms, afraid that if she said anything else now, she'd ruin the magical moment. That somehow, she'd ruin everything.

So they walked along the snow-covered beach, holding hands and talking about the family or the gossip that had gone around earlier.

When it grew too late and too cold, they turned back to the house with the dogs trailing slowly behind them.

"I think they're finally worn out," Jacob said, opening the back door and allowing the dogs to rush inside. "I'll walk you to your truck." He shut the back door again.

When he took her hand, she felt her entire body heat. What she wanted to do was find a warm place to be with him again.

It was hard to explain, but even though she'd only been away from him for a few nights, it somehow felt much longer. Her body ached, remembering what it was like to have him inside her. To be wrapped in his embrace completely.

Opening her truck door, she leaned in the cab and watched him.

He moved in closer and she felt her heart skip a few beats as he reached up and pulled her beanie off her head, letting her hair spill out. She held still as he ran his fingers through her locks.

"I miss you," he said in a low tone less than a breath from her lips.

"I miss you," she agreed, pulling him closer. "Kiss me and make me forget that it's going to be another week before my parents leave."

When his lips touched hers, she melted against him. He marveled at the way he could make her desire almost triple with just a simple kiss.

He chuckled at her when she tried to pull him further into her truck.

"As much as I'd love to... I think it's a little too cold and too cramped in your truck to really enjoy you." He rested his forehead against hers.

She knew he was right, even though part of her desperately wished to ignore reason.

She realized she was even now shivering at the cold that surrounded them.

"Breakfast?" he asked. "Tomorrow morning?"

"Yes." She nodded, swallowing the majority of her desire.

He kissed her once more, quickly, and then took a step back. "I'll pick you up around eight," he said quickly. "We can spend the day together."

She smiled as she nodded, not trusting her voice since she wanted to beg him to come back with her. Or go somewhere they could be alone.

"Tomorrow morning." He turned to go but stopped. "Rose, I love my gift," he said before heading inside.

Driving back to her parents' place, she realized that she had completely lost her heart to the man. No matter what happened now, she was done for. If Jacob decided to break her heart now, there was no coming back from it.

She had only ever loved one person and for the rest of her life, would only love one person. Jacob Jordan.

Breakfast the following morning at the Golden Oar was

nice and filled with visiting with half a dozen family or friends who stopped by their table to say hello.

They technically had the day off, but when Jacob received a work call, they headed up to the trailer. She spent a few hours scouring over her own work while Jacob helped fix a water main pipe that had frozen overnight and caused damage on the main road.

After, they stopped by Baked pizzeria for lunch and, of course, ran into even more familiar faces. They ended up hanging out with Riley, Lilly, and Sara and her kids while enjoying lunch.

Somehow, lunch ended up moving to Riley and Carter's place and they were joined by more of his family members.

Blake and Matthew showed up, along with Suzie and Aiden.

That evening, the second-generation Jordans all gathered around a campfire out in the backyard while the children slept inside.

Rose could remember so many summer night bonfires on the beaches with the same people gathered around. It felt like old times, yet when Jacob reached over and took her hand in his, it felt oddly new.

How many summer nights like this had she dreamed that Jacob would reach across and touch her hand or even just look at her as something more than a sister or friend.

Now, here they were, sitting next to one another, her with a symbol of how Jacob felt about her wrapped around her neck.

The thought made her smile even more as she joked with his family members. She never would have thought that she'd be in this position, but no matter how much she wanted to be alone with Jacob, she knew that she didn't want the night to end.

As with the night before, Jacob left her wanting as he dropped her back off at home shortly before midnight.

"This isn't how I expected the day to go. Or the night," he said, pulling her into his lap.

"Oh?" she asked, straddling him. "Just how did you want the day to go?"

His hands moved up to her hips as he pulled her closer. "Well, I'd hoped to find a nice"—he kissed her—"quiet"—he kissed her again—"movie to watch."

She pinched him as he chuckled.

Then his smile slipped as he looked up at her. "I miss you. I miss being with you. Holding you, touching you."

His hands started moving up her hips slowly. She arched into his touch and moaned softly when he cupped her. Somehow, it felt as if he was touching her for the first time again and wondered if it would always feel like this.

"Rose," he said, pulling away, "go inside."

She stilled and felt her heart sink. When she started to pull away, he held her still.

"I really want to finish this, right here, right now, but... something tells me your parents heard us drive up and..."

She could hear the dogs barking now and groaned. "Right," she said with a sigh as she moved off him.

"I have some errands to run tomorrow," he said as she gathered her things. "But maybe we can talk when I get back?"

She nodded and thought about her own plans for the following day. "We're supposed to go into town and do some after Christmas shopping." It was a family tradition, spending time together in the stores as they hunted for bargains and just got out of the house.

He leaned over to kiss her again. "Good night."

"Night." She smiled back at him before climbing out of his truck.

When she stepped inside the house, she was greeted by the dogs. Her parents were watching television and appeared to not notice her return home.

"How was your day?" her mother asked when she sat down on the sofa. She instantly enjoyed the warmth that was coming from the fireplace.

"It was nice," she answered. "We ended up at Riley and Carter's place this evening and I guess we lost track of time. What did you two kids do?" She glanced between her mother and father.

"Slept most of the day away," her father admitted with a chuckle.

"After he worked," her mother added. "All morning long." She rolled her eyes.

"It was only one phone call," her dad corrected.

"It lasted two hours," her mother said with a nudge.

"I didn't hear you complaining. You were right there on the conference call with me." Her dad wrapped his arms around her mom, who smiled and chuckled as she moved closer to him.

"You two are incorrigible," she said after they kissed in front of her.

She couldn't remember a time when they hadn't been affectionate in front of her. She knew that most children grew annoyed or disgusted at seeing their parents' love, but Rose enjoyed seeing how much they loved one another.

Rose pulled a blanket over her legs. "What are you watching?" she asked with a slight yawn. She was too worked up to go up to bed, but too tired to do anything else.

"A superhero movie," her dad answered with a groan.

"Shut up, you're the one who picked it out." Her mother poked him in the chest.

Settling back, Rose watched the end of the movie with her parents before shuffling off to her own bed. She couldn't stop the dreams from coming or her body from aching for Jacob's touch.

She woke a little agitated and tired since she'd tossed and turned all night long. Still, her dad's homemade blueberry pancakes and two cups of coffee helped her out of the mood.

Sitting in the back of her parents' car as they drove into Edgeview, she continued to think about Jacob.

Pulling out her cell phone, she shot him a text.

"Dreamed of you last night."

She smiled when her phone vibrated with his almost instant response.

"Me too. What was I wearing?"

She smiled as she typed her response.

"Your work boots and nothing else."

His response took a little longer.

"You find that hot?"

"Yes, it's like me dressed in only heels and a G-string kind of hot."

"Okay, I have a new Christmas wish list."

She chuckled.

"You okay back there?" her mother asked.

Shifting, Rose nodded. "Yeah, just... texting."

"Gotta go, let's finish this tonight," she sent Jacob.

"Okay, but I'm gonna want a picture."

She smiled. "You send one to me first."

He sent back a face emoji with its tongue out.

"Was that Jacob?" her dad asked.

"Yes, he had things to do today," she replied as she tucked her phone into her purse.

"Things seem to be going well between you two," her mother said.

"They are," she said with a slight sigh as she played with his gift around her neck.

She knew the entire story of her parents and how they had found one another. Still, comparing her and Jacob's relationship with theirs was just plain silly.

Her mother and father had only known one another for a few months before they had fallen in love. She'd known Jacob her entire life. There were actual pictures of them naked in the same bath together. Then again, there had been a few other Jordans in that same bath, and it had been more like an outdoor swimming pool than a bathtub.

Her parents had sworn that when they'd put the lot of them in the water, they'd all had swimsuits on. But each time they told the tale, they laughed so much that they never finished the story.

Her parents helped keep her mind from Jacob or anything else for the rest of the day. By the time they climbed back in the car and headed back to Pride, her feet and back hurt from walking around all day, and she was looking forward to enjoying the hot tub for a while before heading to bed and calling Jacob.

"We're heading up to bed," her parents told her after they finished bringing in all their purchases.

"I think I'm going to sit in the hot tub and try to relax a little before heading to bed." She kissed her mom and dad before heading up to change into her swimsuit. Before heading down to the basement and the awaiting hot water, she grabbed a bottle of wine and a glass.

When she climbed into the hot tub, she sighed with

relief as the hot water warmed her completely. It had stopped snowing earlier that morning but was just now starting up again.

When her phone chimed, she almost ignored it, but then remembered her scheduled call with Jacob.

Putting down her glass, she glanced at the phone screen.

"Don't scream."

She frowned down at the text from Jacob.

She was about to type a response when movement at the corner of the deck caught her eye. She almost dropped her cell phone in the water as she squealed.

"I said not to scream," Jacob chuckled as he moved forward.

"Jesus," she sighed, trying to relax again. "What are you trying to do? Kill me?"

"No." He smiled and started to remove his clothes as he moved across the patio towards the hot tub.

Her mouth went dry as she watched his impromptu striptease.

When he climbed into the water in nothing but his boxers, she was pretty sure every muscle in her body was vibrating.

"I wagered you'd come out here after a long day shopping." He pulled her close and kissed her. "I also wagered on your parents not joining you. I parked at the end of the drive, so as not to alert the dogs and hiked here," he said between kisses.

"My parents went to bed almost an hour ago," she said a little breathless.

He smiled down at her. "So, do you think we can be quiet enough?"

"Their bedroom is on the other side of the house and…"

She smiled. "They are very sound sleepers. If you didn't wake the dogs..." They both stopped and listened for barking and then smiled when the only sound was the bubbles of the hot tub. "Then I think we're good."

"God, I've wanted you," he said before kissing her again.

His hands moved over her, pulling aside her swimsuit. When his fingers entered her, she arched into his touch and gripped him through his boxers. It took a little more maneuvering to pull them off his hips and she tried not to laugh at the difficulty of the simple task.

Then he was back in her arms and they were skin to skin.

"Rose," he said, pulling her up into his arms.

She straddled his hips as he slowly entered her. Water splashed around them as they tried to find a hold so they could move together.

They had made love in the hot tub before, but not when it had demanded they remain so quiet and certainly not when they'd had such a dry spell.

The urgency with which they moved only heightened each touch, each kiss. Her breathing was labored, and she had to bite her bottom lip to keep from screaming out his name when she felt her release explode from her core.

"My god," Jacob said against her shoulder. "I don't ever want to go another four days without you."

She smiled. "Do you think we can sneak upstairs without waking the dogs?" she asked. "I don't think I'm done with you yet."

He chuckled. "As much as I'd like that..." He sighed, and she knew what was coming.

"No," she broke in, resting her head on his shoulder. "My parents already know..."

"Rose." He pulled back and then cupped her face until she looked up at him. "We've got plenty of time. Besides, we both have an early morning. Work starts back up tomorrow."

"Right." She sighed. "Sit in here for a few more minutes with me? At least until I finish this glass of wine."

He glanced out at the snow and then nodded. Neither of them bothered with pulling on their wet clothes again. Instead, she sat next to him and sipped her wine as they watched the snow fall slowly just feet from them.

"I'm going to have to install a hot tub when I move into my new house," he said with a groan as he shifted slightly, no doubt to have one of the jets hit him just right.

"It is one of the best perks of living here," she replied. She set her drink down and wrapped her arms around him. "You are the first reason."

His hands were back on her hips, pulling her onto his lap again.

"Now you did it," he groaned, and he kissed her as she slid slowly onto him again.

CHAPTER FOURTEEN

It was very difficult to go back to work the week between Christmas and New Year's, but it did help keep his mind off being with Rose. Then again, each night he lay in bed alone, he remembered being with her in the hot tub and knew that everything was going to be difficult until her parents went back to Portland.

He'd officially invited Rose to the large formal New Year's party hosted at the Golden Oar each year. He didn't normally look forward to such parties, but this year, knowing that he was going with Rose changed everything.

Work on the sites shut down early New Year's Eve day and remained closed until the second. He stood in front of the mirror in his tux and groaned. Okay, so he didn't like dressing up like a goon. Still, he had to admit... he turned slightly and held up his fingers in a makeshift gun.

"You are no Bond," his brother said, stepping into the room.

Jacob laughed. "And you are?" He motioned to his brother's matching suit.

"Far more than you are." Conner nudged him. "Bond doesn't have a beard."

"It's not a…" He shook his head. "I trimmed it," he said with a shrug. He knew Rose liked the facial hair and it kept his face warm when he was outside. "Where's your date?" He turned away from the mirror.

"Waiting for us downstairs," Conner answered. "I was sent up here to get you."

The entire family was riding together to allow them to enjoy a few drinks. His father had already agreed to drive everyone home and wouldn't drink that night.

Seeing his parents dressed in formal attire, he couldn't help but smile. This was a tradition as old as he could remember.

Then he noticed Kara standing by the fire in a sleek dress that matched the cast still on her arm. He knew she'd already started physical therapy with her mother and understood that it was going slow and that Kara was still wearing a cast to help the shattered bones heal.

"How are you feeling?" he asked her. "Up for a party?"

She smiled. "So ready." She wrapped her good arm around his brother. "Don't let this cast fool you. I can still dance."

"We'll see," Conner said, holding onto her.

"Are you meeting Rose there?" Kara asked.

"Yes," he answered. "That reminds me. You and Rose's mother, Rob, have a lot in common. Apparently, Rob was shot shortly before they got married."

"She was?" Kara asked.

"Yeah, ask her about it," he said with a shrug.

"That was a nasty deal. I'd almost forgotten about it," his mother said as her father helped her on with her coat.

"We'd better hurry. As the hosts of the party, it wouldn't do for us to be late."

Fitting five full adults into his mother's new SUV only assured him that Pride needed an Uber driver or at least a public bus route.

Especially when three of the adults were easily over six feet tall.

"I don't think there is an SUV built that can hold more than two Jordan men," his mother joked as they all climbed out of the car at the Golden Oar.

The entire restaurant was decked out in white lights. The parking lot was already almost fully packed with cars and there was an actual line out the front door.

"Looks like we're late," his brother said as they moved past the waiting people.

"Hey," several people called out to them as they passed, "it's about time you showed up."

Jacob's father waved at everyone and then made a grand show of opening the doors for everyone in line.

People cheered and moved inside out of the cold. He didn't know why or when the tradition had started, but the party wouldn't begin until Iian Jordan showed up.

When someone tapped on his shoulder, he turned to see Rose and her parents smiling at him. Wrapping an arm around Rose, he followed everyone into the warmth and the party.

After stepping inside, he helped Rose off with her heavy winter jacket. The moment it slid down her back, he froze.

The long gold glittery dress barely had a back to it. Rose's perfect skin kept his attention as she stepped away and turned towards him.

Her long hair was curled in soft waves as it flowed over her shoulders. The dress clung to her like a second skin. Its thin straps dipped lower in front to showcase her perfect breasts. She'd done something amazing and new with her makeup, causing her eyes and her lips to be exaggerated.

She'd never looked more beautiful than she did at the moment.

He took a moment to recover and then said, "You look beautiful." He handed off her coat and his own to the coat check. Wrapping his arms around her, he whispered in her ear. "My god. You look good enough to unwrap."

She giggled and leaned back. "I can't believe how amazing you look in that suit. I've always wanted to attend one of these famous Jordan parties."

"That's right." He snapped his fingers. "This is your first New Year's with us."

"Summers." She shrugged. "You never had any parties outside of the Fourth of July parties."

"Well"—he motioned to the room—"welcome." Then he leaned closer and whispered. "Is it everything you dreamed it would be?"

Her eyes moved over the entire restaurant.

String lights hung from the center of the room and went to every corner of the main dining hall.

Since most of the guests were employees, a large buffet table had been set up where people could eat at their own leisure.

The bar was turned into a self-serve style with champagne and beer chilling in coolers.

Occasionally, an employee would shuffle more food in or refill the champagne. But for the most party, everyone was relaxed and already enjoying themselves.

"Drink?" he asked, putting his hand on Rose's lower back and guiding her to the bar area. He poured her a glass of champagne and grabbed a beer for himself.

"It looks like my parents are already enjoying themselves." She motioned with her champagne flute.

He glanced over and smiled at her parents, who were on the dance floor. His parents were right next to them, enjoying themselves just as much.

"One would think that it's the only time my folks get to cut lose," he joked. "They live for this." He sighed. "Want to dance?" he asked her after a minute.

"Not yet," she said with a slight purr. "Show me around some more."

"Where would you like to go?" He motioned towards the buffet area.

Rose glanced around and then a slight smile curved her lips upward.

"Is there someplace... private?" she said in a low voice.

He felt his body instantly react to her request. His mind, however, completely shut off. When her arms wrapped around his waist, he blurted out.

"I can show you my uncle's office."

Rose smiled and motioned. "Lead the way."

Taking her hand, he walked past all the happy guests, in through the kitchen, past the skeleton crew working the party, and into the very private back office his uncle used on occasion.

The moment he locked the door, Rose was pressed against him. Her lips covering his, her hands pushing his jacket off his shoulders.

"I wanted you the moment I saw you in this," she said, gently laying the jacket over the back of the office chair.

"Rose." He shook his head, wanting, needing, a moment to compose his thoughts.

"Jacob, touch me," she said, stepping back into his arms.

He couldn't have denied her. His hands ran over the

soft material of her dress. The kiss deepened and, after changing positions so that he could pin her against the door, his hands ran down her narrow hips until her dress material bunched in his hand and he could feel her soft skin.

She reached for his zipper and since he knew they wouldn't have much time before they were missed from the party, he allowed the speed.

Then he was inside her, his pants pooled at his feet and her dress hiked up around her waist.

Her heeled feet wrapped around his hips as he pounded into her until he felt her convulse around him. Only then did he allow himself to fall with her.

"I think we broke some sort of record." She giggled softly next to his ear.

"Hm," he said, trying to clear his mind.

"We'll have to do this again, soon," she said, shifting slightly.

His mind finally clicked into gear. He'd taken her against the door in his uncle's office, with half a dozen kitchen staff just outside.

Not only that, but he was sure that when they stepped out into the party again, everyone in the restaurant would know exactly what they had just done.

Especially since all they had to do was look at Rose's face. Her cheeks were flushed, and she had a dreamy look she always got after making love to him.

He smiled. He couldn't help it. He enjoyed Rose's after-sex glow as much as he enjoyed seeing the temper on her.

"What are you so happy about?" she said as she tried to smooth her dress material.

"You," he said, zipping his pants. Her eyebrows arched up as she waited for him to continue. "Just remember when we step outside that door that this was all your idea."

She glanced at the door and then cringed slightly.

"Right," she said and glanced around. "Where's my drink?"

He couldn't remember where he'd set her drink and his beer down. Hell, they hadn't even turned on the light in his uncle's office.

Flipping the switch, he smiled when he noticed the drinks right next to his jacket.

Rose walked over and, after handing him his jacket, downed the rest of her champagne, then took a sip of his beer before handing it to him.

"I think I need a few more of these." She wiggled her champagne flute.

"That can be arranged." He walked closer to her and kissed her until he felt her relax in his arms. "What do you say we grab some food first. I skipped lunch."

"I could eat," she said with a smile.

"If you keep looking at me like that, we may end up back in this office," he warned.

His dick jumped in his pants when she purred, "Promise?"

The rest of the party was pretty uneventful. They enjoyed good food, good friendship, and some pretty hot moves from Rose on the dance floor.

If anyone knew they had snuck out and had a quickie in the back office, no one mentioned it or even hinted at it.

He hated knowing that it would be another two days before he would be back with her. Still, it was a huge weight off him to know that the entire town knew about their relationship.

Now they could actually enjoy being seen in public together, which meant they might be able to go out more often.

Seeing his family so happy and enjoying themselves made him even happier. With Rose by his side, he felt like he could conquer anything.

When it grew close to midnight, he pulled Rose out onto the balcony with the rest of the crowd to enjoy the fireworks that would be set off from the Pride docks.

Kissing her under the lights of the fireworks with the hint of fresh snow in the air was the most powerful moment he'd ever experienced.

He could just imagine his future being filled with more great moments like this. He was nervous about trying to convince Rose that he was the right choice for her life. He knew she had great plans. After all, she'd talked about moving on to bigger and better things once this project was done.

Well, she had talked that way before they'd gotten together. Since then, she'd been silent on the subject of her future. Did that mean there was a chance she wanted to stay in Pride? With him?

His New Year's goal was to get to the bottom of what Rose wanted. And to make sure whatever it was, he would be the one to give it to her.

CHAPTER FIFTEEN

The following weeks flew by. Jacob moved back in with Rose, and they welcomed Sophie to her new home.

The dog took a few days to get familiar with her new surroundings, but after that, she fit right in and grew so comfortable with their schedule that most nights, she was waiting for their evening walks before they were.

Work seemed to double in the weeks that followed the holidays. They were so busy they were unable to have any more days off. Even Sundays were filled with her sitting at her laptop around the fireplace with a dog snuggled up at her feet and Jacob on his own laptop working.

The biggest daily joy she had was the long walks with Sophie and Jacob.

She was interviewing people for a sales position since the job had started cutting into her own work each day when potential buyers stopped by the jobsite and wanted information on the homes.

She had interviewed more than seven candidates and hadn't found the perfect one. That was until Hannah

Crawford walked in. The girl was perfect in every way for the job, down to her stylish heeled boots.

Hannah was the type of woman Rose had always hoped to be herself. Girly. Like, really girly. The kind that carried a purse as a fashion statement instead of a necessity.

Half the time, Rose forgot to bring the dang thing along and only remembered when she was on her period or had something from her big wallet she needed. Her important cards and cash were tucked in the wallet phone case she had.

Sure, Rose occasionally wore a dress and heels, but something told her that Hannah wore them every single day. As a salesperson, the type would benefit the business.

Jacob had been out on site when Rose had interviewed Hannah, and she'd hired her on the spot without consulting him.

After all, Rose knew both Hannah's parents, Luke and Amber Crawford. The Crawfords were one of Pride's most talked about couples. Luke had created Modark, one of Rose's favorite online games of the ones she'd grown up playing. That game, along with several others he'd designed and created over the years, easily made the family one of the wealthiest in Pride, along with the Jordan family.

Why Hannah wanted to work for Rose was beyond her, but the girl seemed very eager and Rose knew from experience that she was very friendly and very outgoing.

When Jacob stepped into the trailer almost an hour after they were scheduled to head home, she could tell he was in a mood. He was covered with dirt from head to toe and mumbling to himself as he wiped chunks of mud from his ears.

She tried not to laugh at the sight he made and itched to

sneak a picture of him, but she figured he'd probably make her delete it anyway.

"What happened to you?" she asked, rushing to hand him a clean towel they kept in the little kitchen area.

"The backhoe broke down and got stuck," she thought she heard him mumble. "We think someone removed a couple spark plugs when we were out for lunch." The last part she heard clearly.

"What?" she gasped. "Someone sabotaged the backhoe?"

"Don't know. Eddie's checking with all his men." He wiped the dirt from his hair, spreading it all over the clean trailer.

"Hey"—she stopped him—"do that outside."

"Actually, I think I'm going to go home and shower." He glanced down at his ruined clothes. He looked down at his watch and groaned when he saw it was covered in mud. Using the towel, he wiped the screen clean and winced. "You didn't stick around here for me, did you?"

"No, I have a few things to catch up on before tomorrow." She kept to herself that that was when Hannah was due to start work. She figured she'd tell him when he was clean and in a better mood. "When I get home, you'll have to tell me how you ended up so dirty."

He sighed and tossed the towel on his desk. "Yeah, I'll see you at home. How long will you be?"

She thought about how much more organizing she had to get done before Hannah could take over the sales part of the job and inwardly groaned.

"An hour," she told him, knowing that if she took any longer, she'd raise his suspicions.

"Sounds good." He took a step closer to her and she held up her hands and narrowed her eyes.

"Don't you..." But it was too late. He leaned in and placed his very dirty lips over hers.

"See you," he said with a smile as she wiped her lips clear of dirt.

Half an hour later she was still smiling as she shut down her computer. How was she supposed to focus on work when even a muddy kiss from Jacob set her insides on fire?

She stepped out into the dark and cold and locked the trailer. She'd heard most of the workers leaving shortly after Jacob had, since the light rain had turned to a downpour shortly after Jacob had left to clean up.

She knew that the security company would be swinging by at regular intervals to check up on the job site, but still took the time to lock the gate behind her as she left.

It wasn't a long drive home, but since she figured to put Jacob in a better mood before telling him she'd hired someone without his input—not that she needed it, but still —she headed into town and stopped at Baked to pick up some dinner. Instead of getting a pie, she ordered two spaghettis and a side of their garlic cheesy bread.

The moment she pulled into the driveway, she knew something was wrong. Jacob's truck wasn't there.

Pulling out her phone, she called him as she shut off the truck. It went to voicemail almost instantly.

She decided to put the food inside and check to see if maybe he'd come home, cleaned up, and then left again. She noticed Sophie begging at the front door to be let out, a sure sign that Jacob hadn't been home yet. Setting the food on the counter, she tried calling him again while Sophie rushed out to do her business. As with before, the call went to his voicemail.

She shot a text off to him, asking where he was.

When no reply came back, she let the dog back in before jumping back in her truck.

Could he still be up at the jobsite? Could she have missed seeing his truck in the parking lot? No. She punched the gas a little more. She was positive his truck hadn't been there when she'd left.

Since the last place she'd seen him was at the site, she drove up there, unlocked the gate and slowly drove around the entire property. She relaxed a little when she spotted his truck outside what would soon be his home. Currently, it was nothing more than a hole with mud and rebar walls.

The rain was coming down even harder than earlier and before she climbed out of the truck, she honked her horn a few times in hopes that Jacob would come walking over the hill towards her.

The longer she waited, the more she worried that she was going to have to get muddy herself. What was he still doing out here?

Pulling her raincoat hood over her head, she slipped on her mud boots and tucked her cell phone in her coat pocket before climbing out of the truck. Thankfully, she'd pointed the truck headlights at the home site, since the flashlight on her phone wouldn't be bright enough.

Calling his name as she walked towards the hole, she shielded her eyes from the rain as she looked everywhere for him.

Still, she had to pull out her cell phone and turn the flashlight on it to see inside the dark hole that would eventually be Jacob's basement.

"Jacob?" she kept calling out as she scanned the muddy bottom. The longer she looked the more her heart race and her fear spiked.

When a flash of green and blue from Jacob's raincoat

caught her eye, she almost dropped her cell phone as she cried out and rushed forward. She almost fell directly into the deep muddy hole. Seeing Jacob lying face down in the mud at the bottom had her scurrying around to try and find a way down to him.

"Jacob?" she called over and over as she frantically glanced around for a safe way into the hole.

After assessing the situation, she realized that her only option was to jump down about five feet into the mud. She hoped that the ground was soft enough at this point to cushion her landing.

Gripping her cell phone even tighter, she took the leap and landed less than two feet from where Jacob lay. Her boots sank deeply into the mud and almost stuck there as she started to make her way towards him. Kneeling, she turned Jacob over and gasped at a large gash on his forehead covered in mud and blood.

"Jacob?" she cried, the rain pelting his pale face. He was unconscious and even though she shook him and called out his name, he didn't move.

With shaky fingers, she felt his neck for a pulse. A jolt of relief washed over her when she felt the strong beat under her fingers.

She dialed nine-one-one on her phone, but could barely hear the dispatcher over the rain as she explained what was going on.

She snapped to attention when the woman asked her to apply pressure on Jacob's wound with something clean. Glancing around, she realized the only thing she had that was clean was her shirt.

Setting the phone down on Jacob's chest, she removed her jacket and shirt, then slid her jacket back on before using her T-shirt to stop the bleeding on Jacob's head.

"Rose?" Someone was calling her name.

"Over here!" she called out and quickly told the dispatcher that someone was there before hanging up. "Over here!" she shouted again before a bright flashlight beam hit her square in the face.

"My god." She knew that voice and waited for Aiden to rush around and, much like she had done moments before, jump into the muddy hole to help her.

"What happened?" he said, kneeling beside Jacob.

"I don't know. When he wasn't at home, I came looking for him and found him here. I think..." She swallowed as she remembered almost falling in herself. Then Aiden removed her shirt to look at the cut, and she winced at the wound. "I think he fell in here."

Aiden glanced around after checking Jacob's pulse and his neck. "The only way out of here is if I carry him out," he said. "I doubt the ambulance workers can get down here with a gurney. Do you think he injured his neck or back?"

"I don't know." She shook her head as tears started dripping down her cheeks, mixing with the rain.

Just then someone else called down to them.

Rose stood, her boots sinking into the mud as three men lifted Jacob's still unconscious body carefully out of the hole. Then Aiden helped her climb out.

As she sat in the back of the ambulance, the mud she was completely covered in started to dry. She sat next to Jacob, who was strapped down to the gurney as an EMT took his vitals and cleaned some of the mud from his face.

By the time she walked into the hospital in Edgeview, following the gurney that carried Jacob, the mud was completely dry, making it difficult for her to walk.

Her entire body was shaking from the cold of the

hospital as people scurried around her, taking Jacob's vitals and checking him out.

She saw them cut his clothes from his body just before she was nudged out of the area and into a waiting room.

Aiden was there on the phone and when he noticed her, he hung up and rushed over to her. His arms wrapped around her.

"Everyone's on the way. I had Suzie bring you a clean change of clothes," he said, holding onto her. "The nurse said you can make use of a shower in one of the empty rooms." He started walking with her down a long hallway. "Suzie should be here with your clothes before you get out. Go," he said opening a door. Inside was a standard hospital room. He motioned towards the bathroom door. "Clean up. I'll be right outside waiting for news."

"I... can't leave him alone," she said softly.

"Trust me, he won't be alone for long." He nudged her. "Go warm up."

Since she was shivering uncontrollably at this point, she stepped into the bright bathroom. One look at herself in the mirror and she covered her mouth as a burst of hysterical laughter escaped her.

She was completely covered in mud. The only clean spots were the whites of her eyes and long streaks down her cheeks where her tears had slid down, cleaning a path.

It took some doing, pulling off her ruined clothes. Since she'd removed her shirt in the pit, she spent most of her time trying to remove her mud-soaked jeans.

The moment she stepped under the hot water, she folded as her knees buckled and more tears mixed with the mud washing from her.

No matter what happened, she was not ready to lose Jacob. Not like this. Not now. Not when so much was at stake. She loved him and she had yet to tell him those words. Why had it taken her so damned long? Why hadn't she just told him?

What was going to happen to her if she lost him? There was no way she was going to be able to go on. That much she knew.

CHAPTER SIXTEEN

There was so much pain. Jacob's head was splitting, and he couldn't remember why. Had he had too much to drink?

He remembered the morning after his cousin's bachelor party. His head hurt more now. Actually, the more he woke up, the more he realized his entire body hurt.

"Hey," he heard a soft voice say close by. Rose. "No, don't move," she said softly. "How are you feeling?"

"Terrible," he mumbled and heard her sigh.

"Yeah, but you're alive," she said, and he felt a soft kiss on the back of his left hand.

Too much in his mind was foggy to register anything more. There was a loud ringing in his ears, which drowned out most of what she was saying.

"What?" he asked when he could focus.

"Do you remember what happened?" she asked again.

"No. Was I in an accident?"

"No, it appears you fell into your new basement yesterday," she said softly.

He turned his head slightly towards her voice and froze. Every ounce of his being went on guard.

"Rose?" He said her name and felt his heart skip. "Are the lights on?"

She was silent for a moment. "Yes," she answered slowly. "Jacob?"

"Can you call the doctor in here for me?" he asked after blinking several times.

He listened as she moved around and then heard her relay his request to the nurse.

Moments later he heard as several people shuffled into the room.

"There's our boy," he heard his mother say. He could hear the stress and concern in her tone.

"He requested to see a doctor," Rose said, from a little farther away. "He asked if the lights were on," she whispered.

"Jacob?" His mother's voice was right beside him.

"Mom, I... take Rose out of the room," he said, closing his eyes. He didn't want her to see him like this, at least not until he knew what was going on. He didn't want to worry her.

The door opened, and he listened as people came and went.

"Afternoon." He knew instantly it was the voice of his uncle Dr. Aaron Stevens.

"Hey," he said. "Is Rose gone?"

There was a slight silence, then Aaron moved closer. "Why don't you tell me?"

Sighing, Jacob rested his head back. "I think I knocked something lose."

"How much can you see?" Aaron asked.

"Does blackness count?" He almost groaned it as his head spun.

For the next hour, he allowed Aaron to run tests. Lots of

tests. None of which Jacob felt like he passed, seeing as he still could only see blackness and each time he tried to move quickly, he got dizzy and almost passed out.

When he heard Rose's voice again, he was lying back down in the bed, his parents sitting beside him.

His mother had let him know that the rest of the family was outside in the waiting room. He quickly told her that he didn't want to see anyone else, and she said she understood but, nonetheless, they were all out there for him.

He listened to his mother talk to Rose quietly for a while.

"I'll stay," Rose said in response to his mother suggesting they head downstairs to grab some dinner.

He wanted to tell Rose no. That she should go home. Take care of Sophie and get some rest, but instead, he allowed her to hold his hand and sit beside him.

"We'll get through this," she said softly when he suspected they were alone.

How? he wanted to ask, but instead he closed his eyes and rested back. He knew it was the coward's way out, faking that he was asleep, but he just couldn't talk to her now. Not when his entire life, their entire life, had been taken away in one single moment.

At some point, he must have really fallen asleep. When the door opened and he heard his mother talking softly to Rose, he woke.

"Go," he said to Rose. "Eat something. I'll be here."

"I'm just going to step out for a few moments," she countered, and he felt her soft lips on his.

How could she know how much that soft kiss meant to him? What it did to his heart. Instead of answering, he nodded.

He heard the door open and shut again.

"Son." His father's voice was nearby.

"Dad?" He moved to sit up only to have the bed start moving to a sitting position for him. His father must have been using the buttons on the bed for him.

Just knowing he couldn't even do that simple task for himself had his heart breaking even more.

"What do I do?" he asked, feeling overwhelmed.

He hadn't realized he was crying until his father's fingers brushed his tears away. He knew that even though his father had lost his hearing at eighteen, he was an excellent lip reader. And since there were still tubes attached to his arms, he didn't have the freedom of movement to use sign language.

"You heal," his father replied. "You adapt," he added. "You live."

"Like this?" His voice rose. "Sight is far different than hearing."

"True, but if what Aaron says is true, this could be temporary."

"Was yours? Didn't they tell you the same thing after your accident?" he countered.

His father was silent for a while, and Jacob knew that his words had hit their mark.

Resting his head again, he thought about everything he'd hoped and planned for. His and Rose's future. Now, it was all gone. Taken away.

"Rose," he said, his voice breaking with emotion.

"Still loves you no matter what. Just like your mother still loves me," his dad said firmly.

He knew it was true, but his heart still ached as he thought about the kind of life that he could offer her now.

"I need... time," he said after a moment. "I need to come

back home to heal when I leave here. I can't be a burden on her. I won't. Can you arrange it?"

"If that's what you want," his father responded.

"It is," he said firmly.

"I'll leave you to tell her when she comes back. Until then, get some rest." His dad's hand touched his. "You look like shit."

He smiled. "You sound like it."

He heard his dad chuckle. "I love you, son."

"Love you too."

By the time Rose and his mother returned, he'd made up his mind completely. He was moving back in with his parents. Sophie would have to stay on with Rose for the time being. At least until he grew more comfortable and confident moving around. He hadn't had time to introduce her to his parents' dogs yet and didn't want to burden them with it yet.

Shortly after they returned, his parents left for the night.

"They're going to kick me out soon," Rose informed him. "But your uncle says he's going to keep watch over you all night and possibly release you tomorrow."

His heart sank at the thought of going home and being a burden to his family. He remembered hearing stories of how his family, after his father's accident, had had to learn sign language and alter their lives.

He could only imagine what life was going to be like for them now.

"Rose," he said, holding out his hand for hers. He couldn't even accomplish the simple task of touching her without her help anymore.

He felt her take his hand and the bed shifted as she sat next to him.

"I love you," she said, leaning closer to him. When her lips brushed against his, he closed his eyes and enjoyed the moment. Maybe this moment would be the last he'd have with her like this.

"Rose." He said her name again and waited until she pulled back. "I've asked my parents if I can move back in with them."

She was quiet. "I can—"

"No." He shook his head lightly. "You have work. As it is, you'll have to take over for me until my uncle can find someone to replace me."

"Jacob," she said, and he heard her sniffle.

He lifted his hand towards her face. She moved slightly and rested her face in his palm.

"Will you watch after Sophie for me?" he asked.

He felt her nod her head. "Of course. We'll be waiting for you to return to us. When you're better," she added.

"Rose—"

"No," she interrupted him. "Don't." She pulled her hand from his. "Don't do this."

"Rose," he said, shifting and reaching out for her. "Things aren't going to be able to be like they were before."

"Your uncle said—"

"I know what he said," he broke in. "He also said that it was just a chance my eyesight would come back."

He would have given anything to see her face. To know if she was hurting as much as he was. But he knew this was for the best. Really.

"Jacob, I'm not giving up on you," she said softly.

Just then there was a knock on the door and a nurse came in and informed Rose that she had to leave for the night. Before Rose left, she leaned in and placed a soft kiss on his lips. He felt and smelled her tears and held back the urge to wrap his arms around her and tell her everything would be all right.

Spending the night alone, in the darkness, was the most difficult thing he'd done in his entire life. His uncle came in several times to check up on him and told him that he'd stayed behind to keep watch over him for the family.

"I'm giving your parents hourly updates," Aaron informed him.

"How am I progressing?" he asked dryly.

"You have a lot of swelling," Aaron said. "Your head looked like an oversized marshmallow before, now you're down to a regular sized marshmallow."

He held back a chuckle. "It feels like one. I've been avoiding moving or breathing too deeply."

"The hope is that when the swelling goes down, your eyesight will come back." His uncle sighed. "The brain cells you lost when you turned Rose away I doubt will ever come back."

"You heard about that?" He groaned.

"Your family is worried about you. We're willing to do whatever it takes for you to recoup, but pushing any one of us away in your time of need..." His uncle made a tsking noise. "Not a good choice, if you ask my opinion."

Aaron's words left him thinking for the rest of the night. He continued to play over what little he could remember of the previous day.

He knew it was morning when he smelled the fresh coffee brewing down the hallway. He felt his stomach growl and hit the nurse call button.

When his parents walked in some time later, there was a tray of food sitting in front of him.

He never realized how hard it was to eat food you couldn't see. In the end, he'd only eaten the toast dry and drank the coffee black. He almost spilled it several times before he learned not to set the mug down between sips.

"How are you feeling today?" his mother asked in a chipper tone.

As a response, he groaned and held his head.

"Sorry," his mother said in a whisper. "You have visitors today."

"Who?" he asked.

His sister replied, "Your twin. You know, the one you refused to see yesterday. Do I need to remind you that I'm pregnant and upset at you?"

He felt her sit on the edge of the bed before she leaned in and hugged him.

"How are you feeling?" Riley asked in a soft tone.

"Hungry," he replied. "And wanting to go home."

"Well, I can help you with one of those. I brought donuts," Riley answered.

"Godsend," he said, holding out his hand for one.

Riley set a donut in his hand and then leaned in. "Rose is here," she said softly.

His smile slipped slightly. "Do you have coffee?" he asked. "The stuff they gave me earlier tasted closer to the goo you clean out of the bottom of the mug."

Riley chuckled. "Hold out your other hand. Sara made your favorite just for you. It might be a little cold from the drive."

"It could be frozen, and I'd still drink it." He took a sip of the lukewarm drink and sighed with joy at the sweetness. The donut tasted much better than the dry toast he'd had earlier.

"Who else is here?" he asked Riley.

"Your brother," Conner said. "And Kara," he added quickly.

"We could only have a few people in the room at a time. The rest of the family is waiting outside," his mother said. "Aaron says that after he comes in and checks up on you this morning, he may send you home."

"That's good news," he said, and somehow felt Rose's eyes on him from across the room.

CHAPTER SEVENTEEN

She couldn't stand it for much longer, knowing that Jacob was going to be going home and doing this all alone. She wanted to be with him. Wanted to help him.

But she could see the smarts to his plan. After all, just spending the last couple days at the hospital was setting the work on the site back. She'd asked Eddie, Jacob's right-hand man, to help out and keep the work going, but nothing replaced Jacob.

Nothing and no one ever could.

So, she stood back against the wall as he visited with his family. She doubted he knew that she was there, but shortly after his sister left the room, his head turned in her direction and, for a split second, her heart jumped at the possibility that he could see her.

But then he almost spilled his coffee by trying to set it down on the tray in front of him and her heart sank just as quickly.

She listened as his uncle came in and examined Jacob. He ran a few tests and informed them all that Jacob was free to go home.

She watched his face closely and could tell that Jacob was relieved and a little upset at the same time.

She wanted to go to him but remembered how he'd pulled away from her last night. She'd cried herself to sleep, holding on to Sophie.

He was making the conscious decision to leave her. To let this be the thing that divided them.

She'd told him last night that she loved him, and he'd told her he was moving back home. She knew that it was probably hard on him, but she had to believe that he was going to get better. She just had to.

Even if he didn't, her feelings for him weren't going to just magically disappear. She'd loved him for far too long for that to happen.

"We brought you some clean clothes," his mother said after Aaron left the room. "Do you need help."

"I'll help him," Rose jumped in.

She watched his eyes move in her direction. He didn't seem surprised, which meant he'd known she was there all along.

"We'll be in the waiting room." His mother handed her the bag she'd packed up with his items earlier.

"You didn't have to..." he started as he shifted to sit up on the edge of the bed.

"Don't," she warned him as she started to untie the hospital gown. "You need a shower. There's still mud on you everywhere."

"There is?" he asked.

Instead of answering, she took his hands and pulled him to his feet. "Come with me."

He followed her like a drunk man, stumbling, not lifting his feet, and holding out his free hand as if he didn't trust her not to walk him into the wall.

Standing in the bathroom, she finished untying his gown and let it fall on the floor. He didn't flinch or even blink as she ran her eyes over him.

How many times had she enjoyed his body? The lean toned muscles that ran over every inch of him.

Currently, there was still dried mud on parts of him along with a massive bruise that ran down his left shoulder and ribs.

Her fingers gently traced the outline of it while his breath hitched.

"You have a bruise here," she said softly. "You must have gotten it when you fell into the basement."

"Rose." Her name sounded so good from his lips.

"I'll turn on the shower." She stepped away from him. When she turned back to him, after the water had warmed up, she watched as he stood in the middle of the bathroom, unmoving.

Taking his shoulders, she led him into the shower.

"There's soap." She took his hand and rested it on the container of liquid soap on the shower wall. "The emergency call button thingie." She took his hand and moved it to the left. "Don't accidently pull it. I'll be right here if you fall."

"You don't have to."

"Shut up." She smiled. "I'm enjoying the view. Now, clean." She handed him a washcloth and stepped back out of the spray of the water.

He moved as if on automatic. Closing his eyes, he allowed the water to wash over him. She wanted to warn him not to get his bandage wet but knew that Aaron had mentioned having it replaced before he left the hospital anyway.

Moments later, he ripped the thing off and tossed it to the ground as he finished shampooing his hair.

"You missed a spot," she said, walking over before he reached up to turn off the water. Taking the washcloth from him, she rubbed the dirt from his shoulder blade, moving over his skin slowly so as to not hurt him any further. When his skin was clean, she reached up and turned off the water and then took his shoulders again and led him out. Then she wrapped a towel around his hips. He took the towel away from her and tucked it firmly around him.

She grabbed another towel and started drying his exposed skin. A low hiss escaped his lips.

"Rose, where are my clothes?" He practically growled the words.

"Come home with me," she said. She looked into his eyes and saw no response. Her heart sank slightly as sadness threatened to surface. "Come home. Let me and Sophie take care of you."

"No." His hands gripped hers firmly and pushed them away. "I can't do that to you. I won't do that. Give me my clothes."

Stepping back, she handed him the bag. "If you need help."

"I won't," he said quickly.

She stepped back and watched him dress slowly. When he was done, she walked over and touched a clean cloth to his head, which was starting to bleed again.

"You'll need a fresh bandage over this before you leave." She dabbed the cloth gently to stop the bleeding.

He winced and she pulled the cloth away. "Sorry."

She called the nurse into the room to put a new bandage over his cut and waited and listened to his discharge information. The nurse wheeled him out to meet his parents in the waiting room.

Then she watched them drive away and part of her heart went with him.

What was she going to do now? How was she going to live without him?

Every fiber of her being wanted to be there with him, helping him. Taking care of him.

Instead, she drove back to the job site and went back to work.

She'd put Hannah's first official day off and before she'd left the hospital had sent a text to her telling her to meet her at the trailer in an hour.

Now more than ever, she'd need the woman's help. Especially if she was going to fill Jacob's role and her own. Indefinitely.

When Hannah stepped into the trailer, she had a bundle of flowers in her hand.

"My parents, for Jacob." She set them down on the table. "How's he doing?"

"He's at home. Resting," she answered.

"Alone?" Hannah asked.

"His parents' home," she corrected.

"Oh, well, that makes sense. I mean, you do spend a lot of time here at work," Hannah said with a slight frown.

"It's a stupid idea. His stupid idea," Rose said, crossing her arms over her chest. "His worst idea by far."

Hannah moved over and sat across from her desk. "Trouble in paradise?"

"Hannah, how long have you known Jacob?" Rose asked her.

Hannah laughed. "Well, let's see, he's about five years

older than I am, so..." She held up her fingers and pretended to count before nodding. "All my life."

Rose smiled. "You're witty. It's another reason I hired you," she said, pointing at the woman. "Okay, so I get that he's experiencing something new." Rose sighed and shook her head. "Losing your eyesight. I can only imagine how scared he must be. But I'm supposed to be there. With him. Helping him. When something scary happens, you call the ones you love to lean on. Right?"

"I guess." Hannah shrugged slightly.

"You guess?"

Hannah shifted in the chair. "I mean, men think different than women. I know that when my dad broke his collarbone a few years back"—she rolled her eyes—"racing a damned kid's bicycle through town. Anyway, when he was injured, he pushed my mother to her breaking point. I mean, he didn't want her to do anything for him. He said he didn't want to be a burden on her or anyone else."

Rose thought about it. Is that what Jacob was doing to her? Pushing her away because he didn't want to be a burden on her.

She remembered how he'd been when she'd helped him in the shower and cringed. Maybe he did just need some time.

She knew she hadn't been clingy or overhelpful. Actually, Aaron had prepared everyone for what Jacob would be going through in the next few months. The anger, the denial. The anger.

She'd listened carefully and had wanted to be there for Jacob during all of it.

"I can see by the look on your face that you think that's what he's doing," Hannah said with a sigh. She tapped the arms of the chair. "Well, boss lady, what's my first task?"

For the next few hours, she showed Hannah the ropes. Since Jacob wasn't using his desk, she gave Hannah free range of changing the space up. She even helped her move all of the samples into the sitting area and organize everything.

Hannah claimed that prospective buyers should see all the wonderful choices right as they walk in the door. Not some disorganized office.

Then they moved Jacob's stuff into her office and arranged the two desks to face one another.

"There, now this is better. People coming in will be greeted with beautiful choices. Are you going to have a model home?"

"Yes," Rose answered. "It will be on lot one." She motioned to the large map of the proposed subdivision she'd had made up.

"Wonderful. A lot of builders fill the model home's garage with all these samples. You know, have the office there as well."

"Yes, it's what's planned." She smiled. "You really do know your stuff."

"Oh." Hannah chuckled and waved her hand. "Every time I go into the city, I go home shopping. Not that I'm looking to move. Or buy a home." She shook her head. "Okay, truth be told. I'm a new home junkie. I live for walking through homes. Seeing floor plans. Seeing all the pretty decorations they shove into homes. I have never missed a Parade of Homes." Hannah leaned closer. "Never."

"I knew I liked you. Like recognizes like." She pointed her thumb at her chest. "I'm a Parade of Homes superfan myself."

Somehow being with Hannah helped take her mind off of Jacob. Still, it loomed over her like a dark rain cloud.

While Eddie organized the men outside, she coordinated everything from placing orders to when shipments of material would arrive.

For the next few days, she was so busy, she couldn't afford to focus on anything else other than work.

She couldn't even text Jacob and when she tried to call him, it went to voicemail. She doubted he had even plugged in his phone. Or that he knew where his phone was. She'd called his parents but each time she talked to his mother, she claimed Jacob was resting.

"I should be there helping him," she told his mother.

"Rose," Allison had said, "I feel your pain. He has barely left his room since coming home."

"What can we do?" she asked her.

Allison had sighed heavily. "When Iian lost his hearing, he pushed everyone close to him away."

"When did it change?" Rose asked.

"Jacob just needs time. He loves you. I know he does. Everyone knows he does. He just needs time."

So, that's what Rose gave him. An entire week went by before Allison had called her. An hour later, she knocked on the Jordan's door. Sophie sat at her feet, eager to meet the barking dogs that responded to the doorbell.

"Rose." Allison answered the door wearing a painter's smock splattered with bright colors. "Sophie." Allison knelt down and scratched the dog's head before opening the door all the way for the three dogs to happily greet one another. "We're out back enjoying the sunshine while it lasts."

"Jacob?" she asked, removing Sophie from her leash since it appeared that the dogs were going to be friendly with one another.

"Iian dragged him out of his room earlier. He begrudgingly is sitting on the back patio sipping a beer while Iian has been playing with the dogs and I'm painting." She leaned closer. "Thanks for coming."

Rose nodded, not trusting her voice as she followed Allison through the house to the back patio.

Seeing Jacob sitting in a chair, holding a beer, had her heart doing a flip in her chest. He no longer had a bandage on the cut on his forehead. Instead, a small bandaged covered the spot. Most of the swelling on his head had gone down as well. His hair was a little longer, and she realized that he must not have cut it since before the New Year. He needed to trim his beard. It was twice as long as usual and very shaggy.

Sophie made a beeline past the two dogs and rushed to almost climb up in Jacob's lap while making a happy whiny sound.

"Hey," Jacob smiled and loved the dog.

"Rose has stopped by with Sophie," Allison said cheerfully.

Rose watched Jacob's smile slip slightly as he continued to pet his dog.

"She missed you," Rose said, moving closer to Jacob.

"I wasn't sure she'd get along with the other two," he said, pulling the bigger dog up into his lap. "Okay, girl." He laughed and held onto Sophie, who was whimpering. "Okay." He buried his face into her fur.

"How are you feeling?" Rose asked and watched Jacob wince. She knew better than to ask, but she needed to know.

"Still blind," he replied dryly. It stung, but she tried to let his sarcasm pass. "How's work?" he asked as Sophie settled on his lap like it was the softest bed in the world.

"Busy." She took a seat across from him. "Enjoying your time off?" she asked, wanting to get a rise from him like he'd gotten from her so many times before.

She watched the side of his mouth twitch. "Yeah, it's just another day in paradise."

"Well, anytime you want to come back..." She let her words hang. "Oh, my new employee has moved your desk into the office with mine."

"Employee?" he asked. "What employee?"

"I hired Hannah Crawford as a sales associate. To greet and deal with potential home buyers. I figured I'd need the help since I was stuck doing both our jobs."

"You're trying to piss me off," he said in a soft voice.

"Maybe." She smiled. "Is it working?"

He took a deep breath and then shifted Sophie in his arms.

"How about a walk?" she suggested. "Sophie's been locked up all day, and she could use stretching her legs."

"Rose," he said, but Sophie had heard the magic word— walk—and quickly jumped out of his lap. She danced around Jacob, eagerly waiting for the walk Rose had just promised her.

"Okay," Jacob said when Sophie nudged his leg. "I'll go."

Rose smiled and quickly clipped Sophie's leash on her pink collar and then handed it to Jacob.

"Thank you," Allison mouthed to her as the three of them started heading towards the beach. It was a nice wide pathway, and Rose guessed that Jacob would have less of a chance of tripping on things walking on the beach than if they'd headed towards the pond. But that didn't mean she was going to make this easy for him.

CHAPTER EIGHTEEN

"How is Hannah working out?" Jacob asked once they were on the beach.

Rose hadn't helped him once, but since Sophie was doing a good job keeping him on the pathway, he'd only stumbled a couple times. The moment his feet sank into the soft sand, he bent down and unleashed the dog and whistled, his signal that she was free to run.

He'd heard his mother holding back their two dogs and figured she knew that they would be too much for them to handle. This was, after all, his very first outing since returning home.

"She's the best thing that's happened to me in a week," Rose said easily as she draped her arm in his and started walking quickly down the beach. "When are you going to come home?" she asked. He had to shift slightly to keep up with her. The sand was uneven, and he didn't want to trip and fall. Not in front of Rose.

"I've been thinking about it," he said, a little winded. "I've asked my uncle to release me from the contract. It's not possible for me to purchase my own place now," he admitted.

"Jacob?" She jerked his arm until he stopped walking. "You can't give up your entire life."

He dropped his arm and took a step back. "What I can't do is see. I can't even brush my own teeth anymore." His voice rose slightly. He was angry. Angry at his own inability to do the basics in life. "I can't find my shoes. I can't match my socks. I can't even see this." He motioned around them. He could hear the waves lapping on the shore, but everything was just blackness. The entire world was right in front of him and he couldn't enjoy it. "It's all just... nothing." He closed his eyes on the pain.

"There are lots of people in your same position," she said softly. "They live just fine. They learn. Go to school. Hold jobs. Fall in love. Get married. Have kids." She walked into his arms. "We'll learn together."

He remained stiff as she held onto him.

"I can't do that to you. Not to you," he said, taking her shoulders and pushing her away. "I won't do that to you. To anyone." He'd made up his mind. She was too good for a life helping him live.

"What about your parents?" she asked. "Do you know how much your mother and father have sacrificed their entire lives for his disability? None. Not one ounce of their lives has been placed on hold or cancelled."

"That's different." He threw up his hands.

"Why? Because you say so?"

"My dad can find his way through the house without breaking things," he retorted.

"And you can learn to as well," she supplied. "With some help."

"From you? You just said you've been very busy at

work. When are you going to teach me?" he asked. "What am I going to do all day while you're at work? How am I even going to pay bills?"

"I'll..." she started, but he stopped her.

"No." He shook his head. "Rose. This has to end. We can't keep fooling ourselves. This isn't going to work. Take me back." He whistled for Sophie, who rushed back over to him.

When he felt Sophie next to him, he bent down to clip the leash back on her. He felt her wet fur and knew that she'd been playing in the water. Sophie had always loved the water when they had gone on walks. "Home," he said to the dog, but she didn't move.

"She's confused. She wants to go to our place," Rose supplied. "She keeps looking down the beach towards what she thinks of as home. This way, Sophie," Rose said gently. Sophie followed Rose, pulling Jacob along with her.

He had to let it sink in. Over the past week, he'd thought of nothing but Rose. Of what her life would be like if he allowed her to care for him. In every scenario, he knew he couldn't do that to her. He wouldn't subject her to such torture.

She stopped him by touching his arm. "You know that I love you. Right?"

Just hearing the words from her again had his heart breaking even more. He knew what he had to do. He knew it was for the best. For both of them.

"I can't." He shook his head.

"I know you think you can't. I get that. But soon, you'll realize. You'll come to your senses, and I'll be here. Right here waiting for you."

He felt her brush her lips against his and for a moment,

he almost melted. Almost relented. Then Sophie jerked slightly, and he almost toppled over.

Rose didn't stick around long after they returned to the house. His parents had moved inside because a chill had settled in. Ever since he'd been home, he'd only been out of his bedroom to shower and eat.

After Rose left, he sat and listened to a game with his dad since he didn't want to ask his father to walk him back upstairs. It was almost ironic—he could only hear the game, and his father could only see it.

He figured he'd wait for his mother to come back down from her art studio to deliver him through the house.

But upon hearing his dad's light snore, signaling he'd fallen asleep in front of the television, he didn't want to wait any longer and slowly started making his way back up to his room.

He only tripped three times and bumped into two tables. There had been plenty of times in his life that he'd believed he knew the house like the back of his hand. Now he realized he didn't know it as well as he'd thought.

It was as if he was in a stranger's house, unable to even know where the simplest lamp sat in his room. He kept forgetting about the one between his bed and the desk and had on many occasions, bumped his knee on the heavy thing.

Lying in bed, he didn't even remove his shoes and no longer cared for any of his comforts. Or his mother's sheets.

He woke sometime later when he heard the dogs barking and listened to his father let them out before coming upstairs and heading to bed.

Feeling frustrated and bored out of his mind, he sat up and thought about anything he could do. There was nothing. He couldn't even surf the internet any longer.

He thought of the book he'd been reading at Rose's place. He'd never get to enjoy the ending and find out who had murdered the old woman. Then he thought of all the books he'd miss out on.

He knew his mother listened to audiobooks, but he had never downloaded the app on his phone. Hell, he didn't even know where his phone was at this point.

Closing his eyes, he tried to think of anything he could do for a living while being blind. He knew his job wasn't possible.

What did blind people do for a living? He itched to do some research on the subject, but oh yeah, he was blind.

The more he thought about it, the more frustrated he grew.

Hell, he couldn't even go for a walk if he wanted to. The last thing he wanted to do was get lost and have search parties out looking for him like some lost little kid.

"Restless?" His mother's voice sounded from the doorway.

"I thought you went to bed?" he asked.

"I was about to when I noticed your light was still on."

"It's a habit to turn it on when I come into the room," he said with a shrug.

He listened to her walk into the room and take his arm. "Come with me," she said, and he followed her down the hallway.

He knew the moment they stepped into her art studio. The smell of paint and paint thinner hit him. It was an oddly soothing smell.

"How many times have you come into this room, begging to watch me paint?" his mother asked.

He smiled. "Too many times," he admitted as she moved him over to help him sit at her desk.

"Here." She handed him a paint brush.

"What am I supposed to do with this?" he asked with a laugh.

"Get out your frustrations. You know how I keep my colors." She handed him the pallet. "Red is at twelve o'clock, yellow at three, blue at six, and white at nine," she said. "There's a fresh canvas in front of you." She held up his hand and ran the brush over the canvas.

"Mom." He shook his head. "This is stupid."

"No, it's not. Paint. You always had a talent for it. Just... let your feelings out. Who cares what it looks like? You can't see it anyway," she said with a slight chuckle. "Jacob. Paint," she said a little more softly.

Taking a deep breath, he dipped the paintbrush in the paint and then, closing his eyes and opening his mind, he tried to recreate what he imagined in his head.

His mother sat there silently watching him as he painted.

He lost track of time as he worked. Lost track of everything as he asked for more colors. More paintbrushes. Asked for his paintbrushes to be cleaned or for other tools.

When he'd worked all his frustrations out, he set the tools down and asked his mother.

"Well?" He waited for what seemed a full minute before she responded.

"It's... amazing," she answered.

"Are you crying?" he asked, a little shocked at the sadness in her tone. "Is it that bad?"

She laughed before responding. "You can't deny a mother her emotions when she sees that her son has so much talent. Even if he can't see how beautiful it is."

"It's Rose," he said softly. "God, I hope she never sees this."

His mother's hand rested on his shoulders. "Think you can do another one?"

"Well, since I've done nothing for the past week but sleep and I'm bored out of my mind..." He shrugged. "Why not. Hook me up with a fresh canvas."

He spent the rest of the night working side by side with his mother. He didn't know what she was working on, but on the next canvas, he painted Sophie. Or at least he tried to paint her. He could clearly see in his mind what he wanted and used his fingers to trace an outline before filling everything in with bright colors.

"It's Sophie," his mother said over his shoulder.

"Okay, I guess it's good enough to at least recognize that much." He set the brush down.

"She's blue," his mother said.

"I know. The last time I saw her, we were walking back to the house in the moonlight," he responded. "It's what I remember. Seeing the moonlight reflect off her tan coat."

"It's beautiful," his mother said. "Why don't we get a snack? Your father baked some brownies earlier. There's some vanilla bean ice cream left over."

"Lead the way." He stood up and took a moment to stretch his back. He'd been sitting longer than he'd thought and was sore. Then he held out his arm for his mother to take.

Sitting around the kitchen table while his mother heated up a brownie and scooped up ice cream reminded him of his childhood. The sounds, the smells. He could just close his eyes and know what his mother looked like moving around the space.

She was probably wearing a pair of her flowing yoga pants and a paint shirt with bright colors splattered all over it. No doubt her long hair was up in the sort of messy bun that his father always teased her about.

"Did I ever tell you about the day I fell in love with your father?" she said as she set something down in front of him. Her hand wrapped around his as she handed him a spoon. "Careful, it's hot," she warned.

Reaching out, he took hold of the bowl and scooped a bite of brownie into his mouth. The ice cream was melting on top, and he moaned at the richness of the caramel mixed into the chocolate, along with the vanilla of the ice cream.

"I've heard the story one or two times," he replied. "How you came back into town to visit and how Grandma wasn't well."

"No," his mother sighed, "I fell for your father long before I left Pride."

"You did?" he asked, scooping another bite.

"Yes," she replied with a sigh. "I fell for him, really fell for him, the day he kissed me after taking me to my spring formal." She sighed again and he almost rolled his eyes. "It was months before his eighteenth birthday and the accident."

Jacob stilled, knowing instantly where this was going. "Mom."

"Shush, I'm telling a story," she said quickly. "Anyway, we went to a dance, and he walked me up to the front porch and kissed me." Another sigh and this time he did roll his eyes.

"Seriously? Mom." He groaned.

"A few weeks later, he went on the boat trip with his father. I never stopped loving him. Not when he was throwing things at Todd and Lacey. Not when he stopped talking out loud for years. Never. When someone earns your heart, there is little they go through that you don't go through yourself. So I added American Sign Language to my skills, and I waited and hoped that, one day, your father would come to his senses."

"He would have been a fool if he hadn't," he admitted.

His mother was silent for a while. "Rose has loved you for as long as I can remember. That little girl used to take all the crazy things your cousins would do to her and brush them off. But not you. The moment you played a trick or teased her, she took it to heart. She used to follow you around like you walked on air." He heard her chuckle. "Rob and I used to joke that one day we'd be in-laws." His mother's hand took his. "You kids were ten at the time."

He took her hand in his. "Mom, I can't put her through something like this."

"Have you asked her what she wants?" his mother asked.

"It doesn't matter."

"Yes, it does. Take it from a woman who waited too damn long for the idiot she loved to come around. It does matter." His mother tapped his hands. "Now, I'm tired and heading up to bed." He heard something scrape across the table. "Your cell phone. It was left in your truck. It's charged." He heard her get up. "You know how to use talk to text. Don't be as big of an idiot as your father was."

He listened as his mother made her way upstairs.

Pushing his empty plate aside, he took his cell phone and tucked it in his pocket. Then he immediately pulled it out again.

"Text Rose," he said after hitting the side button.

When it beeped at him, he took a deep breath.

"Thanks for coming over today," he said, and then he said, "Send."

His phone beeped and he hit the button again and asked it to read his message.

"Rose sent you a new message. *We miss you. I'm glad you have your phone back. I miss talking to you.*"

He smiled when the phone rang.

"Hello?" he answered quickly.

"Hey," she said softly. "You're still up?"

"Yeah." He leaned back in the chair. "And since my mother just plied me full of sugar, I'll probably be up for a few more hours."

"Oh? Do you want some company?" she asked.

"Don't you have work tomorrow?"

"Tomorrow is Sunday," she answered quickly.

He frowned slightly. How had he lost track of the days? Then again, it was almost impossible for him to know.

"Feel up for a drive out here?" he asked, thinking about being with her again.

"I can." He heard her shifting around. "For you."

"I'd like that," he said softly.

"Give me ten minutes."

"Come to the back door. I'm in the kitchen," he said before she hung up.

He waited, almost counting the soft sound of the seconds ticking by on the clock that sat on the mantel of the fireplace in the television room.

He heard her truck pull up and smiled when a soft knock sounded at the back door.

Walking carefully, he made his way over and unlocked the door.

Rose walked into his arms immediately. Her mouth fused to his as he shut the door behind her.

"Rose," he said softly.

"No, don't talk, Jacob. I don't want to talk now." She

pulled on his shoulders until he followed her across the room. "I hope to god your mother is a deep sleeper."

He chuckled. "She claims she wears ear plugs since my father snores. Since he can't hear himself, he denies it."

Rose chuckled as she pushed him down to sit on the sofa, then straddled his hips. Her mouth was back over his and, he had to admit, not being able to see her, to only use his other senses, was kind of hot. He smelled everything about her. Her shampoo, the fabric softener that she used. The sweet scent of some flower perfume she wore. Then his hands moved to her hips and the soft fabric of yoga pants against her skin had him moaning in delight.

His hands slowly traveled upward until he cupped her breasts.

"You didn't even put on a bra," he groaned as he enjoyed pinching her nipples between his fingers.

"I was kind of in a hurry." She arched into his hands. "I want you," she said with a groan. "Now." She tugged on his shirt.

"God, you smell so good," he purred.

"You smell like paint." She chuckled as she pulled his shirt over his head. "It's kind of sexy."

His hands moved over her, pulling her own clothes off, tugging on the yoga pants until she sat over him, fully unclothed, and reached for his jeans. "Tell me you have a condom here."

"I think there's one in my back pocket," he said shifting.

"Yes," she exclaimed, and he relaxed back as she slowly slipped it on him.

"My god, you feel so good." He ran his hands over her skin, cupping her, holding her as he moved his hand lower and slid his fingers in and out of her.

"I don't want this to stop," she said, sliding down onto him fully.

"No," he agreed, holding onto her hips as she rocked over him.

All he could do now was hold onto her as she took what she wanted from him. He felt her release, felt her body tighten around his and knew that, no matter what happened to him in the future, nothing would compare to the feeling of Rose coming for him.

Stars exploded in his head as he felt his own release shake his entire body, melting his core and the walls he'd put up over the past week.

When her body went lax over his, he pulled the blanket that always sat on the back of the sofa over their bodies and wished more than anything that he could see her one more time.

CHAPTER NINETEEN

Rose heard her cell phone alarm go off. Thankfully, before falling asleep in Jacob's arms, she'd been wise enough to set an alarm so she would wake up long before his parents would.

The last thing she wanted to do was be caught naked in their TV room like some teenager.

"What?" Jacob said, rolling over and pulling his arms tighter around her. She wiggled free to find her phone and shut off the alarm.

"I set an alarm so I could leave before your parents got up," she said.

"Smart," he sighed against her hair. Then he pulled back with a jolt.

"What?" She frowned at him.

"Rose?" he said, shaking his head slightly.

Her eyebrows shot up. "Did you forget who you spent the night with?" she teased.

"Rose," he said again, then he reached up and ran his hand down her face. "You're a brownish blob."

She gasped. "You mean... You can see me?"

"Not everything. Mainly colors." He squinted. "Some shapes." He smiled. "But yes, it's not all black any longer."

He sat up and rubbed his hands over his face then blinked a few more times. "It's like looking through lenses with Vaseline on them." He wiped his eyes a few times. "But I can see." He turned back towards her and smiled. "I can see you smiling at me."

She jumped into his arms and kissed him.

"Just what I wanted to see first thing in the morning," Iian Jordan said from the doorway. "My son's naked ass."

Rose gasped and yanked the blanket up around her own naked body.

Jacob laughed and turned to his father. "I can see," he exclaimed. Iian, after reading his son's lips, let out a strange sound and then rushed to his son and hugged him. While Jacob was still very naked.

Rose's cheeks burned as she hunted quickly for her clothes. She had never been more embarrassed in her life. Nor did she ever think she would top this moment.

After she'd tugged on the shirt and yoga pants that she'd been wearing when Jacob had texted her last night, Allison rushed into the room.

"What's going on?" she asked, holding her robe against her body.

"I can see," Jacob exclaimed. "Not fully, but..."

"My god!" Allison said, then shielded her eyes quickly. "So can we, and we see everything you were born with. Put on some clothes." She waved him away.

Jacob laughed and rushed over to slip on the jeans that Rose held up for him. He easily took them from her hands, which meant he could see her holding them. She smiled again.

"You really can see." She hugged him after he slipped his jeans on.

"It's getting better." He sighed into her hair. "My god." She felt him shake in her arms. Rose felt more arms wrap around them and looked to see his parents holding onto them both.

"This calls for a special breakfast," Iian said. He stepped away and then headed to the kitchen.

"I..." She wiped tears from her eyes. "Sophie," she said suddenly. "I'm going to go..."

"Why don't you head back and grab her and bring her back here?" Allison asked her with a smile.

Rose glanced towards Jacob. "I'll ride along with you." He glanced around. "Help me find my shirt."

His mother walked over and picked it up from the dining room floor and held it out for him. "After breakfast, you get to clean up," she said with a smile. "Go, get your dog. Breakfast will be ready when you return."

The moment they stepped out the back door, Jacob took a deep breath and took a moment to glance around.

"My god, I never thought I'd see this again. It's all so... amazing," he said after a moment.

"How are you feeling? Do you have a headache or anything?" she asked once they were in her truck, heading to get Sophie.

"No, last night, after"—he glanced at her—"I had a slight one, but I just believed it was... from something else." He shook his head. "I slept better last night than I have since the accident."

"Maybe you just needed the rest?" she suggested.

He reached over and took her hand in his. "I think I just needed you."

Her heart did a little flutter. "I'm happy you texted me last night."

"So am I," he said as she parked by his truck.

"My truck," he said with a smile.

"Your brother delivered it from the job site the day after your accident."

His smile slipped slightly. "Until I'm back to one hundred percent, I think I'd better leave the driving to you."

"You should probably go see the doctor. You know, to get checked," she suggested.

"If I know my parents, my uncle will be waiting when we return for breakfast," he said as he climbed out.

She could hear Sophie barking to be let out and stood back as Jacob rushed to let her out. Watching the reunion was the sweetest thing she'd seen in a long time.

It was as if the dog knew he was different than yesterday.

"If you don't mind, I'll head in and take a quick shower and change," she said, and stepped inside.

"I'll take a short walk with Sophie while we wait." He placed a kiss on her lips.

She rushed up the stairs, showered quickly, and pulled on a clean pair of clothes. She took a few moments to apply some makeup and braid her wet hair.

When she stepped downstairs, Jacob was standing at the back door with Sophie at his feet.

"How are you feeling?" she asked, wrapping her arms around his waist.

"This view," he said with a shake of his head. "I never really stopped to appreciate it before."

She glanced out the window and smiled. How many times had she stopped and just enjoyed the view herself?

She could only imagine seeing it after a little over a week of darkness.

"Rose." He turned towards her and wrapped his arms tightly around her. "I'm sorry I pushed you away."

Shaking her head, she held onto him. "You were afraid you'd be a burden." She pulled back and looked up at him. "You were wrong," she added with a smile.

"Yes, I was," he agreed. "For that I'm sorry."

"If there is anything that's going to get between us again—"

"There won't be. Nothing is ever going to make me turn away from you again," he promised her.

He'd been right. When she pulled into the driveway at his parents' place, there were four other cars parked where there hadn't been any earlier.

"For what's about to happen, I'm sorry," he said with a smile.

She leaned over and kissed him. "Nothing can embarrass me more than your father seeing us this morning."

He chuckled. "That was the most embarrassing and most enjoyable moment of my life."

She nodded in agreement. "Let's not have many more moments like it."

"Agreed." He took her hand. "This will be good. I promise."

True to his word, the moment they stepped in the back door, Jacob was engulfed by his family. Conner and Kara were there, as well as Carter and Riley. His uncle Aaron and Aunt Lacey were as well, and Aaron requested a few moments alone with Jacob to examine him.

Rose stepped into the other room with them and watched as his uncle once again examined him, this time coming back with a nod and a smile.

"Good. You've made so much progress. Headaches?" he asked.

"Some, nothing too bad."

"Eyesight still fuzzy?" Aaron asked.

"Yes, but it's getting better."

"No driving. No working heavy equipment," Aaron said and Jacob nodded in agreement. "And I'll want to see you in my office Monday morning before you head back to work."

"Agreed. Now, how about some food. I'm starving," Jacob said with a smile.

"Well, I'm super thankful you're better," Aaron said, shaking his hand once again.

"Me too." He nodded in agreement.

How many times had she sat around this very table and eaten with the family? More than a dozen times over the years. Yet, somehow, this breakfast felt like the biggest celebration of all of their lives.

Laughter echoed throughout the house. Iian had outdone himself cooking up a storm for the family. She hadn't planned on spending the entire Sunday there, but soon, morning turned into lunch, more of his family stopped by, and suddenly everyone was out on the patio grilling out and playing with the dogs.

After eating lunch, Jacob stood up and held out a hand for her. "Walk with me?"

She eagerly took it. This time, all three dogs followed them down the pathway to the beach.

When they reached the soft sand, he pulled her down to sit in the sand next to him.

They sat in silence as they watched the dogs play in the surf.

"What's next?" she asked.

"Now, we go home." He took her hand and looked at it as if he was studying it. "We finish building our new home. Together."

Her heart did another one of those flutters and then melted. "Together," she agreed.

"Rose, I know that I messed things up."

"Don't," she interrupted.

"No." He turned towards her. "We both know it. I don't know if I can ever make it up to you for pushing you away, but with a lifetime ahead of us, I'm damn sure going to try."

She smiled. "I think I can get behind that."

"So, you'll marry me?" he asked.

She glanced sideways at him and felt her entire body flutter. "Is this the best you can do?"

He chuckled. "I didn't want to wait. I should have planned something grandiose, but I couldn't wait. We've waited too long already." He pulled her into his lap, and she laughed as the sand went everywhere. "I should have asked you to marry me back in ninth grade, when you showed up at the Fourth of July party wearing that knockout red swimsuit." His eyes traveled over her face.

Her heart did another little flutter, this time filled with relief, just knowing that he was able to see her.

"I wore it to get your attention. I'm so happy to hear ten years later that it worked," she purred as she leaned down for a kiss.

"So? Are we finally going to make our families happy?" he asked.

"So now it's about what our families want?" she joked.

His smile slipped slightly. "It has never been about them. But it is a perk getting our mothers to stop meddling." He reached up and cupped her chin. "Rose, I should have told you how I feel about you long ago."

She held her breath, waiting for the words she'd dreamed of hearing from him her entire life.

"You are the only woman I've ever dreamed of being with, of spending my life with. I doubt I can ever make it up to you for pushing you away. Something tells me that whenever we fight, you won't let me forget it. And I can freely say it right now, I deserve it." A chuckle escaped her, causing him to smile even more. "I live for moments when I can rile you up. I find it extremely sexy, just as much as seeing you wearing that sexy red bikini. Please tell me you still have it?" She nodded quickly and laughed when he said, "Thank god."

She shifted slightly on his lap. "You used to annoy the hell out of me."

His smile grew. "And I'm not going to promise to stop anytime soon. So, let me be very clear. If you agree to marry me, you get me as I am. Irritants and all. Think you can handle me?"

Smiling, she remained silent as she thought about their future together.

"I suppose it could work," she said slowly.

He chuckled. "Going to make me work for it?" he asked.

"You made me work for years." She leaned in and kissed him. "I think you can come up with something that would impress even me." She kissed him again, this time slower and with more passion.

"Deal," he said between kisses. "I guess we can move onto the next item. Can we make it official? Say it's our home we're building together, me, you and Sophie?"

"Yes!" She almost shouted it as she hugged him and kissed him again. This time, her shout of joy caused the dogs to scurry towards them and rush around them as if it were a game.

When they walked back to his parents' house, they were all covered in sand and mud.

"We'll have to wash the dogs outside." He motioned to the shower area.

Washing Sophie was one thing, but washing Snoops and Sneak was another. By the time they were done drying all three dogs off, she knew exactly where the two brothers had gained their names. Neither of them wanted to sit still for any length of time. Snoops kept sticking his nose everywhere while Sneak would quite literally scurry off and try to hide.

"They hate bath time," Jacob said with a laugh. "It's why they spend a lot of time in the laundry room." He opened the back door to let the dogs in. "If you'll wait, I'll go upstairs and get my things so we can go home."

"That sounds great." She held onto him when he wrapped his arms around her and kissed her again.

"Oh, there you are," Allison said, causing Rose to jump away from Jacob. "I wanted to show you something." She walked over and took Rose's hand and started leading her down the hallway.

"Mom, we were about to head home," Jacob said.

"You have time." Allison waved her son off as she continued dragging Rose towards the stairs.

A few moments later, Rose stood in front of two paintings, speechless.

"I had no idea Jacob could paint," she said again.

"If he's this good when he was blind, imagine what he could do now?" Allison said with a sigh. "I was floored when he did these last night. Part of me believed I'd been dreaming."

"They're amazing," Rose said, looking at the bright colors of her own face staring back at her. Sure, her face was bright pink, but you could tell that it was the reflection of the sunset she was looking at. The colors behind her show-cased the beauty of what the scene in front of her eyes must be like. Then she turned to the one of Sophie and had to sit down. How had he captured so much of the dog's person-ality in one scene?

Sophie's soft tan fur was a bright blue with orange high-lights. White snow lay all over the ground and Rose got the hint that a full blue moon hung somewhere overhead. Sophie's eyes were full of love and excitement as she looked into the soul of the viewer.

"I love them," Rose said softly as she wiped a tear from her cheek. "Has he seen these yet?"

"Mom? Rose?" Jacob called out.

"In here," his mother called out.

Rose stood back as Jacob stepped in. After taking in what they were looking at, he groaned.

"You showed those to Rose?" he said with another groan.

"Honey, you need to see them." His mother took his arm and nudged him into the room. "I want to show them to Ric."

"Jacob, I've been raised around art my entire life." Rose stepped forward. "I can tell you without a doubt that these are amazing. Not only amazing, they are some of the best I've seen." She glanced towards Allison. "Present company aside."

Allison waved her off with a smile. "Look. For the first time, look at the talent you have."

Jacob stopped in front of the two pieces, and Rose watched his frown slowly dissipate.

"Well?" Rose asked him after a moment.

He turned to her and smiled. "They look just like I

imagined they would when I painted them." He glanced over at his mother. "Thank you."

"For the talent?" she replied back.

Jacob laughed. "For everything." He dropped his arms from around Rose and walked over to engulf his mother in his arms.

CHAPTER TWENTY

Being home was one of the best feelings in the world. Aside from being able to see again.

Falling asleep with Sophie at his feet and Rose wrapped in his arms was where he wanted to be for the rest of his life.

Which had him thinking about his official proposal. What the hell was he going to do to impress Rose?

He knew the way he'd asked her earlier had been lackluster, but he'd been desperate to start their new lives together. If he had his way, they'd have the shortest engagement and marry at their earliest convenience. But he knew that all women wanted something more grandiose.

After all, Kara and Robin made a whole business out of putting together some of the fanciest weddings ever.

He wondered what kind of wedding Rose would want. Sure, most days she was wearing a hard hat and work boots. But just the memory of her in the dress she'd worn for New Year's had him remembering that she was very girlie underneath the rough show she put on.

Which of course put him in the mindset of planning

something amazing for her. Smiling, he plotted everything out in his mind as she slept next to him.

The following day, he had to stop by his uncle's clinic before heading to the jobsite, which meant Rose was going to be late for work.

"Don't worry about it. I've given Hannah a set of keys, and she'll make sure that the gate is unlocked for the workers," Rose assured him.

Sitting in the waiting room at the clinic in Pride reminded him so much of his childhood. He couldn't remember there ever being a time when he didn't feel at ease when he'd been sick, knowing that he was in good hands or about to feel better after a visit with Aaron.

Besides, when he'd woken up, his eyesight had been back to one hundred percent. Being with Rose was the best medicine he could ever ask for.

"I'd like to schedule you for another scan, but if the headaches have disappeared..."

"They have," he agreed.

"Then I think we can wait until you're caught up on work," Aaron finished. He turned to Rose. "If you promise to let me know if there are any concerns and don't let him overwork himself."

"Promise," Rose said quickly.

"Ganging up on me?" he asked, with a smile for Rose.

"If that's what it takes," she replied, making him laugh.

"Okay, I promise," he told his uncle. "Can we go now? I'm dying to get back on the jobsite."

"Go," Aaron said with a sigh. "Make homes." He waved him off.

He couldn't remember ever being this anxious the first day on a jobsite. But stepping back out in the muck of things, he felt as if he was born for it.

He felt as if he hadn't left at all. Or at least he would have if there weren't a million things to catch up on.

He was thankful that Eddie had taken the reins while he'd been gone. The man was very grateful that Jacob was back on the site though, as he had told him many times during the course of the day.

"I'm not cut out to be the boss man," Eddie said with a laugh. "Too much stress."

"Tell me about it," he said, rubbing his sore back. "I was gone just a little over a week and now I feel like I just did all the work myself." He rolled his shoulders.

"I never did hear how you ended up falling in a hole you knew was there?" Eddie asked him.

He hadn't really thought about it before. He'd been too preoccupied with losing his sight to focus on why he'd even gone out to the site. Rose had told him that he'd stopped by the trailer and told her that he was heading home. So, what had changed his mind? Why had he driven up to his home-site instead?

Since it was on the way back to the trailer, he stopped by his future homesite and walked around.

The muddy mess had been cleaned up and now where there had only been bare rebar walls to the basement, full cement walls were finished. He was lucky he'd fallen into soft mud instead of the hard cement.

Later that week they would be framing out the main floor and the rest of the house. Soon, it would start looking like a home instead of just a hole.

He couldn't figure out why he'd returned there that night. Maybe he'd just wanted to walk around? Check out the work. After all, the men had just finished digging out the basement and had installed some of the supports for the basement walls.

From what Rose had said, he'd been covered in mud and the rain would have been a deterrent to keep him away from any freshly dug basement.

So then why did he stop by here? He walked slowly around the site and finally gave up just as the sun was sinking behind the water.

Climbing back into his truck, he took one more glance at the site and froze as a memory played in his head.

He'd been taking one last look around the jobsite before heading home, making sure all his men had left for the day. Then he'd spotted a flashlight beam, and he'd pulled over and gone to see if one of his men had forgotten something.

He'd been heading towards the beam of light when he'd heard a noise behind him and turned to see what it was. Then everything had gone black.

"Son of a bitch," he growled as he headed towards the trailer. Pulling out his phone, he called Aiden and let him know what had happened.

When he stepped into the trailer, Rose and Hannah were giggling at something. Just hearing the joyous sound had him wishing he wasn't thinking about new dangers around the jobsite.

"Hey," Hannah said with a smile. "We were just talking about you."

"Oh?" he asked, sitting on the edge of Rose's desk. He had to admit, he liked the way the two of them had rearranged the trailer. Just the fact that his desk now faced Rose's made it easier for him to work during the day.

Rose's smile slipped. "What's wrong?" she asked him before he could say anything else.

"Aiden's on his way up here," he said with a sigh. "I remembered something. I didn't fall into the basement. I remember being hit from behind."

Rose gasped slightly. "Someone... attacked you?"

He nodded.

"Who would do such a thing?" Hannah asked.

His eyes moved to Rose.

"You think it was Carson?" Rose asked.

"There were two of them. One was ahead of me with a flashlight while another came up behind and hit me," he answered. "Whoever it was, they were sneaking around the site. Which means every single jobsite needs to be double-checked before moving forward."

"We just had our inspection on lot seven, your brother's lot, today and it passed with flying colors," Rose said.

"So we check out all the other sites, including ours. That's where I ended up, so that's where we start."

"Agreed. If someone has been sneaking on site after dark and messing with things, we'll need to know," Rose said firmly.

"It's too late tonight to check things out. The sun is going down, but first thing in the morning." He broke off when Aiden stepped into the trailer.

For the next half hour, he relayed everything he could remember to Aiden. He started to get a headache and grew extremely tired after going over it all again.

"You're tired," Rose said touching his shoulder after Aiden and Hannah had left.

"Yeah," he agreed, "and hungry."

"Why don't we get out of here. Todd's agreed to double security around here. Let's head in, grab a pizza, and take it home and eat it in the hot tub?"

He gripped her hips and pulled her into his lap. "That sounds wonderful."

Less than an hour later, he hissed slightly as he sank

into the hot water. A cold beer and the pizza sat on the edge, out of the way of Sophie's reach.

Rose was still inside, changing. He'd brought out a bottle of her favorite wine and a glass she always drank from.

He was going to wait for her to eat but sipped his beer as the bubbles and heat started to relax his tension.

Then she stepped outside, and the beer bottle almost slipped out of his hands. The small red bikini clung to her every curve. Her long dark hair was piled on top of her head.

Setting his beer down, he helped her climb into the water and pulled her directly into his arms.

"For me?" he asked her.

"It still fits," she said with a smile.

"You may not be wearing it for long," he warned, causing her to smile.

"Long enough to get some food?"

"I can't make any promises," he said, and he kissed her.

The following day was even more stressful. He had to stop all progress to get every worker on site to check and recheck the work that had been done. When they started finding issues, he'd believed it was just sloppy work that had been done while he'd been gone. But the mistakes were piling up and by the end of the day, there was a long list of jobs that would have to be redone in order for three homes to pass any of their next inspections.

"Son of a..." He tossed the list down and felt like kicking something. Instead, he sank down into the chair and laid his head down on the cool wood.

"Headache?" Rose said, coming up behind him and rubbing his shoulders. He moaned and took several deep breaths to try and relax.

"We'll get through this," she said softly.

"It's going to not only set us back but cost us." He groaned.

"We'll get through it. Now that we're on to them, maybe we can set a trap?"

He sat up. Why the hell hadn't he thought of it himself?

"That's not a bad idea." He turned towards her. "We'll need some help."

He pulled out his phone and started calling his family. In the end, he decided to have a family meeting at his parents' place later that night for dinner. He shot off a text to his dad, who said that he'd contact the rest of the family members.

After heading home and showering and changing into clean clothes, Rose, Sophie, and he headed back over to his parents' place.

"Weren't we just here?" Rose joked as the dogs greeted Sophie at the back door.

"I'm sorry." He turned to her. "Did you confuse my family with someone else's?" He laughed. "If you really are going to agree to marry me, you'll have to get used to being over here a lot." He bent down and kissed her.

"And it's a good thing I get along great with all of them," she replied with a smile. "I was talking to the dogs," Rose pointed out with a chuckle. "They appeared to have missed one another." She motioned to the three dogs running around as if they hadn't seen one another in years.

He laughed. "Right." He took Rose's hand and stepped into the house.

The following hours could only be described as organized chaos. Ideas were shouted out at the dinner table while Rose jotted down notes.

The ideas were narrowed down, argued over, and finally, in the Jordan tradition, voted on.

"So, it's decided." Todd Jordan, whom technically was the head of the clan, stood at the head of the table. "Josh will install state of the art security cameras around the job site, and we will get Aiden to schedule some drive-bys."

Jacob's frustration grew and he stood up. "This doesn't set the trap we were all hoping for."

"No, it doesn't," Todd agreed. "But what it does is keep everyone in this family safe." Todd's eyes moved around the crowded room. "And that, at the moment, is our top priority. Especially after your injury."

Rose took his hand under the table, which oddly settled him down and he relaxed back and listened to the rest of the family's plan.

Driving back home, he was too weary to argue any longer and actually had started to see the upside of his family taking over. They had more time than he did, since he and Rose were busy focusing on their work. Also, he had a grand reproposal to plan out. The way he was thinking, if he was lucky enough, by Valentine's Day, they would make their engagement official.

CHAPTER TWENTY-ONE

Rose sat back and waited, each day hoping that the videos would capture legal evidence to lock someone away. Even if it wasn't Thomas Carson.

If she ever got her hands on the person who'd hit Jacob over the head and dumped him in a mud hole, she'd... well, her mother didn't raise no wimp.

For as long as Rose could remember, Rob Derby had taught her daughter how to defend herself. Rose had earned her black belt in both tae kwon do and jujutsu before she'd graduated middle school. Not that she'd kept up her studies —don't tell her mother—but she still did occasionally do some basic stretches when she needed to be more limber.

Every day she logged into the website that Josh had given her when he'd set up more than a dozen hidden cameras, and every day she watched them only to see nothing. Okay, she saw a few deer graze on a cleared lot and a beaver drag one of the cleared trees away and even thought she spotted a mountain lion once. But so far, no humans hell-bent on destruction.

She could tell that even Jacob was growing frustrated at not catching someone doing something. Sometimes at night, he would go off and work on his laptop downstairs alone. She didn't know what he was working on but figured that he didn't want her to know about it.

Since Hannah had started working with them, she'd sold two more homes and had three more potential buyers trying to pick out the right home plan and lots before signing on the dotted line. Hannah was definingly paying off.

The free time Rose had allowed her to help Jacob coordinate the work and the repairs that needed to be done. Repairs that had put them back two weeks on the sites that had been affected.

She'd been so busy working that when Jacob asked her what her Valentine's Day plans were, she'd been shocked at how much time had gone by.

How had she lost an entire month?

"I don't have any plans," she replied. "Did you have something in mind?"

"Yeah, I figured we'd head down to the Oar," he said with a shrug.

Not that she was complaining, but having dinner at his family's restaurant wasn't top of her romantic ideas list. Actually, on average, they ate there at least once or twice a week.

But since she hadn't even remembered that the special date was coming up, she figured it was better than nothing.

"Sure," she said quickly. The least she could do was go dress shopping and pick out an outfit that would stop his heart. "I think that would be a great idea."

She'd also have to find something special for him while she was out shopping.

"Great." He had bent down and kissed her. "Then it's all settled."

"Yes," she said with a nod. The rest of the day had gone off without a hitch. That following Monday, she told Jacob she had errands to run and convinced Hannah to play hooky and go shopping in Edgeview with her. She really did appreciate the girl's sense of style. Maybe Hannah would help her improve her wardrobe.

Rose knew that she wasn't the girliest of girls. It wasn't as if she was a complete tomboy. But facts were facts. She worked on a construction site every day. For her to get the idea that she could wear fancy clothes and pretty things was just not practical.

Still, her closet had as many dresses and high heels in it as it did jeans and work boots. She actually liked and looked forward to putting on nice things and making herself feel sexy for Jacob.

She remembered how he'd enjoyed the dress she'd worn on New Year's.

Hannah took her to a few stores in Edgeview she'd never stepped foot in before. The prices were twice as expensive as any outfit Rose had ever purchased.

Not that she minded spending the money, but when she could, she always tried to stay within a budget.

But since she figured it was going to be a special occasion, her and Jacob's first Valentine's together, she guessed that if she found the perfect dress, she wouldn't complain about the cost.

When she tried on the little pink dress, both she and Hannah knew that it was the one.

It had off-the-shoulder puffy sleeves and clung to her waist before jutting out into a perfect knee-length flare skirt. She found matching heels and jewelry to accent the entire theme of the night. The pink heart diamond that Jacob had given her would go perfectly with the entire ensemble.

"You should wear your hair up, like this." Hannah showed her a photo as Rose drove them back to Pride.

The girl in the picture's hair was curled in tight little ringlets with the front of the hair braided to the side and tied up while the rest of the hair fell over her left shoulder.

Rose laughed. "I can barely manage a braid sometimes."

"Oh, this is easy. I'll send you the video link on how to do it yourself." Hannah pulled back her phone and started typing. "There." Rose heard her phone chime with a new message. "Done."

"Thanks," she said, pulling into Hannah's driveway. "Thank you again for coming along with me today."

"No problem," Hannah said, grabbing the bags of items she'd purchased from the truck. "Gosh, I miss shopping for someone else."

Rose chuckled. "I can tell." She motioned to the many bags.

Hannah laughed. "Hey, I needed some new clothes for work. Thanks for the day off, boss."

Rose nodded. "You earned it. Thanks again for helping me out."

"Have fun tomorrow night," Hannah said as she waved goodbye.

On her way home, she decided to swing by the jobsite. Knowing it was late, and that Jacob had probably already gone home, she figured she'd just ensure that the gate was locked up tight.

Seeing the gate wide open, she pulled in and parked next to Jacob's truck.

Finding the trailer empty, she called him and heard his

cell phone ring inside his truck. Worry instantly caused her entire body to vibrate as she called out his name.

Then she heard the shouting and ran towards the voices.

"I said, what the hell are you doing here?" It was Jacob.

Rose turned the corner of the trailer and saw Jacob holding a man by the scruff of his jacket.

"Like I said, I was looking for work," the other man replied.

"Is there a problem here?" Rose asked, getting Jacob's attention.

Just then, the man swung out and kicked Jacob in the knees and barley missed hitting him in the head. Rose cried out, worried that Jacob would injure his head again.

Jacob, being caught off guard, folded and landed on his knees in the dirt.

Rose jumped forward, blocking the man from striking out and hitting Jacob in the face.

The man was roughly Jacob's size but twice as thick, which meant she was seriously overpowered. Still, she'd practiced enough moves to know how to take an unsuspecting man down.

"The problem is," her mother had said during one of her first self-defense classes, "that men don't view most small women as a real threat." This particular time, her father was her mother's unfortunate sparring partner. "Use that." Her mother wiggled her finger at her father, and Rose watched as he jerked towards her. Her mother had moved so fast that before Rose could understand what had happened, her father was flat on his back, panting and smiling as he looked up at her mother.

Rose still had a firm hold on the man's fist, the one she'd

stopped him from plowing into Jacob's face. Using all her will, she relaxed slightly and allowed the man to believe he had the upper hand.

Jacob was still on his knees, and Rose knew that before he could get up, the man could easily overpower them both.

She waited until she felt the man's muscles tense as he prepared to strike, and then she moved. Using his own weight and inertia against him, she managed to get the man lying on his back in the dirt a few feet away.

Jacob recovered quickly and scrambled to hold the man down.

"Call Aiden," Jacob said to her quickly.

Pulling out her cell phone, she dialed Aiden's number and hastily explained what was going on.

"Don't move," Jacob told the man.

"Move? I can't even breathe," the man said. "I was just looking for a job."

"Tell that to the cops," Jacob said back to him.

"You assaulted me." The man shifted and tried to get up.

"I said"—Jacob shoved his knee into the man's shoulder —"don't move."

When Rose heard the police sirens, she rushed to the front of the trailer and waved Aiden to where Jacob still held the man down.

"I saw him messing with the power." Jacob motioned towards the trailer. "He claims he was just here to apply for a job."

"I was," the man countered as Aiden hauled him towards the patrol car in handcuffs. "I just wanted a job."

"Are you okay?" Rose asked, walking into Jacob's arms.

"Yeah." He kissed the top of her head. "Remind me to

never piss you off. I'd forgotten you could lay a man out so quickly." He chuckled.

"Thanks to my mom." She sighed.

Aiden returned. "I'm going to haul him down and question him. I'll have Josh forward me the recordings. We'll see what he was up to before you two came along."

Jacob nodded. "Hey, if there's a clear shot of Rose's impressive move on the guy, shoot me a copy."

Aiden's eyebrows shot up. "Oh?"

Jacob chuckled. "Just watch it." He hugged Rose tighter. "We're going home."

"I'll call you later," Aiden promised. "Either way, we have him on trespassing."

"Thanks," Jacob said.

A little over an hour later, while they were sitting in the hot tub eating leftovers, Jacob got a text message from Aiden and, after reading it, laughed.

"Aiden says anytime you want a job at the precinct, you've got one. Impressive moves." He showed her the image of her flipping the man earlier.

She'd never really watched herself quite like that before, so at first, she was a little shocked. Then she laughed when the image turned to slow motion. Someone had added a few Batman Pow bubbles and then circling birds appeared above the man's head.

"Nice digital effects," Rose said with a chuckle.

"No doubt Josh's doing." Jacob laughed and set the phone down. "What can I say, it's hot when you know your woman can take down a man double her size."

"Your woman?" Rose shifted to hover over him, her arms blocking him in. His smile grew as his hands shifted to her hips. "Your woman?" she asked again, a little slower.

"If you'll agree to it," he said smoothly.

"Is this your second attempt at proposing to me?" she asked, moving slowly over him and feeling what she was doing to him, enjoying what being so close to him was doing to her own body.

"No," he said softly. "You'll know when I propose again." He reached up and kissed her.

EPILOGUE

There was little Jacob wouldn't do for Rose. Especially after seeing her walking down the stairs in the little pink number.

She'd done something new and fancy with her hair and her makeup. His eyes traveled down to her feet and the high heels that she wore, which were nothing more than small straps of material.

His mouth went dry at the sight of her.

"Wow," he said when he swallowed and found his voice. "You look..."

"How did you put it? Like someone threw up Pepto Bismol on me?" she asked with a smile.

He shook his head. "You have fully redeemed this color in my mind." He wrapped his arms around her. Seeing the small pink heart that he'd purchased her around her neck, he smiled.

"Ready?" he asked.

"Yes," she said with a smile.

They rode to the restaurant in silence. He'd seen the disappointment in her eyes when he'd mentioned where he was taking her for dinner. The surprise, he hoped, would be worth it.

The parking lot of the Golden Oar was packed.

"Wow, I guess you guys are really busy on Valentine's," she said as he helped her out of the truck.

"Yeah, it was a good thing I had connections to get us reservations tonight," he said with a chuckle.

They stepped inside, and he took her hand as they were led towards the back of the building.

"What's this?" Rose asked, stepping into the makeshift room. Black drapes had been hung up to partition off a section of the restaurant.

"This is another perk of having connections," he said smoothly. He pulled the curtain aside so she could step into the private room.

Every ounce of the space was decorated in pink and black. Bright pink rose petals were carefully placed all over the black tablecloth and floor. Roses of matching pink were in vases on the table, which was set for two with tall lit candles.

He helped Rose sit down in a chair before sitting down across from her.

"For you," he said, handing her a pink rose.

"Thank you." She lifted it to her face to smell. "This is all so wonderful," she said with a chuckle. "We even have the perfect sunset view." She motioned towards the windows.

"I have a few gifts for you," he said, "but they can wait until after dinner."

"No, they can't." She shook her head and smiled. "Give them to me now."

He chuckled. "I'll give you one of them now. The rest, later." He stood up and walked over to one of the black partitions he'd hung earlier that day, covering his first gift to Rose.

Smiling, he lifted the veil on the painting of Sophie.

Rose's smile doubled.

"For you." He tossed the material aside.

"I love it." She got up and walked over to touch the frame his mother had chosen. "I wanted it from the moment I saw it." She hugged him.

"Since you gave me a gift, it's only fair I give you one." She leaned up and touched his lips softly. "I'm not wearing anything under this dress," she purred in his ear.

Closing his eyes, he groaned with desire. "Damn, okay. That's not fair. Your gift is much better than mine."

She chuckled. "Give me another one, and I'll return the favor."

He shook his head. "Dinner first." He ran his hands over the soft material of her dress. "If we don't eat now, you'll spoil the next gift."

"Fine." She sighed slowly, then allowed him to pull out the seat for her again.

Plates of food were delivered to them. He half tasted and enjoyed it, but his mind was so focused on the words he was going to say to her, and the fact that she wasn't wearing anything under the tight dress, that he didn't really taste anything.

Dessert, a chocolate mousse with a pink frosting rose on top, was set in front of them.

Holding up his champagne glass, he waited for her to toast with him.

"Happy Valentine's Day," he said with a smile.

"Happy Valentine's Day," she replied. After taking a sip of her drink, she glanced down at the dessert and gasped.

There, nestled in the perfect frosted rose, sat the engagement ring he'd purchased for her.

"Rose, in case you need another clue"—he stood up and pulled aside the cloth that covered his next painting—"this one I did while I could see," he joked.

He hadn't expected tears to fill her eyes as she slowly stood up and, taking her entire dessert dish with her, walked over to him.

Her eyes moved over the painting he'd done in black and pink. Her hot pink. Rose pink, or so he had come to think of it.

The words "Marry me" were written in bold letters with a silhouette of the three of them in front.

"You included Sophie," she said with a laugh.

He took the dessert from her and held it up. "Rose, please say you'll spend the rest of your life letting me make up for all the terrible things I did to you as a child."

She smiled and gently took the ring from the pastry, then slid it on her finger.

"You're probably going to regret this, because, according to you, I was the grossest girl in the entire world," she said with a smile.

Hearing his own seven-year-old words thrown back at him made him laugh.

"Is that a yes?" he asked.

"Yes." She took the dessert from him and set it down before she walked into his arms. "I'll marry you, Jacob Jordan," she said. And then she kissed him.

ALSO BY JILL SANDERS

The Pride Series

Finding Pride

Discovering Pride

Returning Pride

Lasting Pride

Serving Pride

Red Hot Christmas

My Sweet Valentine

Return To Me

Rescue Me

A Pride Christmas

The Secret Series

Secret Seduction

Secret Pleasure

Secret Guardian

Secret Passions

Secret Identity

Secret Sauce

The West Series

Loving Lauren

Taming Alex

Holding Haley

Missy's Moment

Breaking Travis

Roping Ryan

Wild Bride

Corey's Catch

Tessa's Turn

Saving Trace

The Grayton Series

Last Resort

Someday Beach

Rip Current

In Too Deep

Swept Away

High Tide

Lucky Series

Unlucky In Love

Sweet Resolve

Best of Luck

A Little Luck

Christmas Wish

Silver Cove Series

Silver Lining

French Kiss

Happy Accident

Hidden Charm

A Silver Cove Christmas

Sweet Surrender

Entangled Series – Paranormal Romance

The Awakening

The Beckoning

The Ascension

The Presence

The Calling

Haven, Montana Series

Closer to You

Never Let Go

Holding On

Coming Home

Pride Oregon Series

A Dash of Love

My Kind of Love

Season of Love

Tis the Season

Dare to Love

Where I Belong

Because of Love

A Thing Called Love

First Comes Love

Someone to Love

Wildflowers Series

Summer Nights

Summer Heat

Summer Secrets

Summer Fling

Summer's End

Summer's Wish

Distracted Series

Wake Me

Tame Me

Stand Alone Books

Twisted Rock

Hope Harbor

Raven Falls

For a complete list of books:

http://JillSanders.com

ABOUT THE AUTHOR

Jill Sanders is a New York Times, USA Today, and international bestselling author of Sweet Contemporary Romance, Romantic Suspense, Western Romance, and Paranormal Romance novels. With over 70 books in eleven series, translations into several different languages, and audiobooks there's plenty to choose from. Look for Jill's bestselling stories wherever romance books are sold or visit her at jillsanders.com

Jill comes from a large family with six siblings, including an identical twin. She was raised in the Pacific Northwest and later relocated to Colorado for college and a successful IT career before discovering her talent for writing sweet and sexy page-turners. After Colorado, she decided to move south, living in Texas and now making her home along the Emerald Coast of Florida. You will find that the settings of several of her series are inspired by her time spent living in these areas. She has two sons and off-set the testosterone in her house by adopting three furry little ladies that provide her company while she's locked in her writing cave. She enjoys heading to the beach, hiking, swimming, wine-tasting, and pickleball with her husband, and of course writing. If you have read any of her books, you may also notice that there is a love of food, especially sweets! She has been blamed for a few added pounds by her assistant, editor, and fans... donuts or pie anyone?

facebook.com/JillSandersBooks

twitter.com/JillMSanders

bookbub.com/authors/jill-sanders

Printed in Great Britain
by Amazon

63181247R00130